SHADOWS OVER TARALON

SHADOWS OVER TARALON

Jenny goes to work at Taralon in order to assist Bill Williams in his business and also to look after his three children, who have lost their mother in a car accident. Whilst on a picnic, Jenny is rescued from the river by Wayne, Bill's brother-in-law. Although she falls in love with him, Wayne loses interest in her when she is suspected of doping Taralon's racehorse, Pretty Boy. Jenny has to fight to clear her name – and to win back Wayne...

Shadows
Over Taralon

by

Jacquelyn Webb

Dales Large Print Books
Long Preston, North Yorkshire,
BD23 4ND, England.

British Library Cataloguing in Publication Data.

W ebb, Jacquelyn
Shadows over Taralon.

A catalogue record of this book is
available from the British Library

ISBN   1-85389-991-7 pbk

First published in Great Britain by Robert Hale Limited, 1991

Cover illustration ' Maggie Palmer by arrangement with P.W.A.
International Ltd.

Published in Large Print 2000 by arrangement with Margaret
Pearce

Dales Large Print is an imprint of Library Magna Books Ltd.

Printed and bound in Great Britain by
T.J. (International) Ltd., Cornwall, PL28 8RW

CHAPTER 1

The countryside was flat and monotonous. Jenny stifled a yawn. They had been driving since early morning, and now, several silent hours later, she was regretting her impulsive action in taking on the temporary live-in position of book-keeping and light house-keeping. The man's arrogance had got to her, so she had jumped in feet first.

'If you are sick of being cooped up after your last job, it might be a break from office work,' the girl from the Agency had suggested.

Jenny grinned at that. She had just got back from her first free morning at the beach when the Agency had rung to ask if she was interested in an immediate position of temporary at a country property.

'A bit of paperwork and some light

housekeeping, until the permanent recovers from her accident, or whatever! Can you make the interview by four?'

Jenny had been offered quite a few permanent jobs, but after two years with the Agency she wasn't interested in a permanent position. She liked the challenge of different jobs, and prided herself on her ability to cope with whatever came up.

She left straight away, arriving punctually on the stroke of four at the foyer of the city hotel. However, the man who had moved forward to introduce himself as Wayne Paterson examined her doubtfully, a scowl knotting the black brows in a bar across his cool grey eyes.

'Miss Jenny Fleming?' he asked, and from then on the interview had gone straight down hill, and ended up to be more of a headlong confrontation than an interview. 'I was expecting someone older. You look too young for what is required.'

Jenny took a deep breath, deciding that this job wasn't going to suit her at all. She wasn't into chauvinistic patronising employers. She plunged into battle.

'I'm twenty-two! They didn't specify you wanted to sight a birth certificate!'

'I wanted someone responsible!'

'I'm even responsible,' Jenny returned smoothly.

The anger had started to build, causing her blue eyes to sparkle and her cheeks get even pinker. How dare he be so rude! She hadn't had time to change, and had left home straight away, so she was still in her beach wear; sundress, flat heeled sandals and the wide brimmed sun hat tilted over the two plaits over her shoulders.

The grey eyes of her would-be employer became even frostier at her reply. Jenny got the message he wasn't used to anyone answering him back. He stood up to indicate the interview was terminated.

'There are three children to be supervised, as well as the bookwork, and it is important to have someone with sufficient experience and stamina to cope.'

Jenny stood up. She didn't want the position anyway, but temper and her stubborn streak pushed her into recklessness. Her would-be employer was arrogant and judgemental, making sweeping assessments about her competence on a first appearance. What right did he think he had to flick his eyes over her slender fine boned body so contemptuously?

'My references should speak for themselves, and despite your personal views I do have enough stamina and experience to cope with children.' She let an acid note creep into her voice. 'As you will find it difficult to get anyone else with my qualifications at such short notice, and for such a temporary period I suggest you live dangerously and accept the Agency recommendation to employ me.' That had stung, she thought triumphantly as she watched the ugly red flood into his cheeks. She gazed up at him, keeping her eyes deliberately soulful.

He glared back down at her. His grey eyes

were outlined with black lashes which gave a smouldering intensity to his gaze. She wondered if he was going to erupt in temper, and stepped out of reach as she gave him a dimpled smile and took over firmly. 'I look forward to meeting you back here at six tomorrow morning then.'

She guessed it was his restrained fury which had kept him silent, and she gave a gracious nod as though she assumed it was consent. She had glanced around as she marched away, feeling those grey eyes boring into her back, but he had only given an ironic salute before turning and striding back into the hotel.

The next morning his aloof courtesy was all that could be desired, as he put her case in the boot and opened the door of the big car. Jenny fastened her seat belt. Her hair was tucked up in a tight chignon, and she wore a tailored grey slack suit, and shoes with sensible heels. She had an instant flash of satisfaction when she first arrived, realising he hadn't recognised her behind her sunglasses until she spoke, and then there was the one look of startled awareness, and he retreated behind his silence.

Her reluctant employer looked less overpowering in casual slacks and long sleeved shirt. The breadth of his shoulders under his light coloured shirt made his height less noticeable, but he was still a tall man. He had jet black hair, and this morning the black bars of his eyebrows were raised into an arch over alert grey eyes.

Jenny studied his profile out of the corner of her eyes, as he drove skilfully through the city traffic and along the freeway. He had regular features; high cheekbones, a fairly prominent nose and a determined jaw. His mouth was firm and well shaped, and there were laughter lines around the corners. Jenny revised her estimate of his age. Without the unpleasantly grim mouth and the tension, he looked to be in his early thirties. The firm mouth quirked upwards into a wry grin as he became aware of her scrutiny.

'It's a long drive,' he advised. 'Make yourself comfortable.'

They were the last words he spoke for several hours, and Jenny spent her time regretting her impulsive action in forcing him to accept her as the only candidate for the position. The job was probably going to be unpleasant and boring, and the only thing going for it was the fact it was temporary. Suddenly, he spoke, breaking the silence.

'I'll stop for lunch soon,' he promised. 'Are you hungry?'

'Yes,' she admitted.

That was the extent of their conversation. At the next country town, the car purred to a stop in front of the old fashioned hotel. Wayne Paterson got out and escorted Jenny up the steps and through to the dining room. Jenny sniffed at the aroma of roasting beef and steamed vegetables, and decided she was very hungry. Breakfast had been a sketchy tea and toast.

Jenny didn't let the silence of her employer

prevent her from enjoying her roast dinner and sweets. Her employer seemed less interested in his food, and pushed away his plate without finishing. He waited until she had finished a second cup of coffee before ushering her back to the car, glancing at his watch with a worried expression.

'Are we behind schedule?' Jenny demanded. 'You didn't really have to wait for me to have two cups of coffee.'

'I'm anxious to get back,' Wayne admitted. 'The children need constant supervision at the moment.'

'Your children?' Jenny asked.

'My sister's,' he said flatly. The country was undulating and the road unwound ahead of them. His eyes were watching the road. A tic throbbed at the side of his face, but otherwise it was expressionless. 'She was killed last month in a car accident.'

Jenny was too shocked to risk saying anything. She revised her opinion of the tall man with the worried eyes and tense lines around his mouth. It sounded like a pretty traumatic scene to be involved in. No wonder he was so uptight at the interview!

'Marise was thrown clear, and escaped with a few broken ribs and a broken ankle.'

'And I'm relieving until Marise is well enough to return to work?' Jenny suggested.

'The kids have been a bit of a handful,' he muttered.

'I like kids,' Jenny replied. 'How old are they?'

She was rewarded with a quick glance. 'Well that's something,' he said drily.

Jenny repressed her quick retort. Wayne Paterson's tension and irritability was suddenly understandable, and made him seem more human and somehow vulnerable.

'Tell me about them,' she coaxed. 'It will be less difficult to step in and take over if I know something about them.'

His face softened, and the mouth curved up into a proper smile. Jenny felt herself warming to that smile. It altered his entire face. The cold aloofness and arrogance was gone completely. It was obvious he was a doting uncle to his sister's children.

The car purred along the endless winding road, and the afternoon sun slanted lower. Wayne Paterson's nephews, John and Allan Williams were twelve and ten, and caught a bus to school. Meredith nearly five, was still home all day. The property was called Taralon, and mainly ran beef cattle.

'Gwenda's death seems to have knocked all the stuffing out of her husband Bill,' he explained flatly. 'So the kids aren't settling down at all. I've been staying to help, but sooner or later I have to get back to my own place. The housekeeper Mrs Harris has got enough to do without having to do the books and keep an eye on Merry. Which is why I needed someone to fill in until things settled down.'

'No one can replace your sister, or familiar faces around the place, but I will try my best to be of assistance,' Jenny said quietly. 'It sounds as if it has been a dreadful few weeks.'

'Yes,' he said flatly.

It was dark, and the headlights probed onwards through the darkness. It was shortly after this that the car slowed down, and turned through an ornate set of gates. Jenny sat up. This would be the entrance to Taralon.

Half an hour of winding narrow track, and then over a steep hill. The moon was high in the sky, and on the other side of the hill, Jenny looked down into a cleared valley. There were a cluster of buildings, and the lights of a sprawling house beckoned through the darkness.

Wayne parked the car out the front, and tooted his horn. Three children burst from the house and came tumbling down the steps of the verandah. The little girl reached the car first, and flung herself into the driver's arms as he stepped from the car.

'Uncle Wayne,' she shrieked.

The two boys reached him and just clung. Jenny stretched, opened the door and stood waiting. A stooped figure had followed them down the steps, and also waited. Wayne put the little girl down, and disentangled himself from the clutches of the two boys.

'Jenny Fleming, please meet Bill Williams, and of course Merry, John and Allan.'

'Pleased to meet you Miss Fleming,' the other man said tonelessly.

'It's Jenny,' Jenny smiled, holding out her hand.

'Yes,' the man said absently, not seeming to notice her outstretched hand. 'Mrs Harris has kept tea. Do come in.'

'I'll put the car away, and bring up your case,' Wayne called.

He got back into the car with the three children and drove it around the house. Jenny followed the stooped figure up the steps across the wide verandah and through a screen door which led into a large kitchen.

She stood blinking in the light for a few seconds. The stooped figure was a man with greying tousled hair, and a gaunt hollow cheeked face with pale blinking eyes. The kitchen seemed huge, with a large centre table, and benches around the wall, and a couch with someone sitting on it along the window. A stoutly built woman turned with a smile as they came in.

'Miss Jenny Fleming,' Bill Williams introduced as he pulled out a chair for her. His hand shook as he rested it on the back of the chair. 'Meet Mrs Harris.'

'Welcome to Taralon, Jenny,' Mrs Harris smiled.

The other door opened, and Wayne Paterson came in quietly, with the children following him. Jenny smiled at them, but they ignored her, hovering as closely around Wayne as he would let them.

A husky chuckle came from the couch. Jenny looked across, suddenly aware of the girl on the couch, a plaster cast on one long leg, and crutches leaning against the wall. Her first impression was of dazzle, of white teeth, of gleaming eyes, and shining blonde hair.

'Hello, Marise,' Wayne said. 'Back are you? Have you met Jenny Fleming?'

The hazel eyes under the shining fringe of hair inspected Jenny, and the red lips curled up in a mocking smile. Jenny met her gaze steadily, but she felt the hackles on the back of her neck rise at the contemptuous look. Was her brown hair untidy, and her grey slack suit that shoddy looking?

'Hello, Jenny Wren,' Marise smiled, but her eyes were wary and watchful. 'Where did Wayne find you I wonder?'

'An employment agency, Marise,' Jenny returned smoothly.

Marise lost her mocking, amused smile. She leaned back on the couch, and gave Jenny a long venomous look. Jenny pretended not to see it, but her heart sank.

She was going to have to look after three children who stared at her with wary hostility, and her actual employer was the absent stooped man who didn't seem to see her properly, and to cap it off, she had just acquired the inexplicable enmity of the girl she was relieving, the beautiful Marise.

This particular temporary job was

certainly going to represent a challenge for her competence and ability! Just what had she let herself in for this time?

CHAPTER 2

The next morning, Jenny opened her eyes and stared blankly at her surroundings. Then she remembered. Today was the first day of her challenging new job. She dressed hastily in a long sleeved shirt and slacks, and finished unpacking her case.

At least the room was warm and welcoming. Yellow daisies in a vase on the dressing table matched the gold drapes, and the sun shone in on the polished floor boards. She guessed it was Mrs Harris who had gone to the extra trouble of putting flowers in the room. She sensed she had met a friend in Mrs Harris.

The door opened, and a small wary face appeared. Jenny smiled, but the face remained solemn, big blue eyes curious but distrustful.

'It's Meredith isn't it?' Jenny asked quietly. 'My name is Jenny. Can you show me where the bathroom is?'

The little girl turned in silence and led the way down the hall. Jenny ignored the scrutiny as she cleaned her teeth, and pulled her hair back into a pony-tail.

'Mummy's gone to heaven for a while, and Daddy's been cross for ages,' the little girl announced suddenly.

'Let's go and see Mrs Harris in the kitchen,' Jenny suggested, ignoring the shocking statement delivered in such a matter of fact voice.

The kitchen was as she remembered, and Mrs Harris turned from the large range to give a welcoming smile. Bill Williams and Wayne Paterson sat at the table drinking coffee. Merry made for Wayne to silently huddle against him, still staring at Jenny with wary eyes.

There was no sign of Marise, but of course she had only dropped in for the evening. Jenny had a confused impression of being introduced to someone with equally flashing white teeth and gleaming blonde hair. Marise's brother – what had they called him? Memory returned. It was Tony Bickerton. He and Marise were joint owners of the adjoining property, whatever adjoining was in this land of endless space.

'Can you ride?' Wayne demanded.

'If the horse is quiet enough,' Jenny replied. 'Do you want me to round up stock or something?'

'They've organised a picnic,' Mrs Harris explained as she put a plate of bacon and eggs in front of her. 'Be a good chance to get to know the children. The boys are back at school tomorrow.'

'I came up here to be useful,' Jenny protested.

'There's always tomorrow,' Wayne drawled. He looked amused. 'If of course you think you can cope with a picnic as your first duty, and can you swim?'

'I'm sure there won't be a problem,' Jenny snapped. 'I even have a first aid course in case someone needs resuscitating!' She concentrated on her bacon and eggs, regretting her outburst. Why did this man manage to get under her skin so easily.

'Good,' he retorted. 'The boys want to do some fishing and have a swim. A day out will do them all good. Give Bill and myself a chance to get some work done.' He finished his coffee. 'Enjoy your day,' he said.

He and the older man then left the room. Merry came over and stood by Jenny's knee watching her eat. Almost immediately the two boys burst into the kitchen. John the elder was dark, but Allan's hair was bright red in the morning sun, with matching freckles across his snub nose.

'Are you finished Miss Fleming?' the older boy asked anxiously. 'Wayne wouldn't let us wake you, and the day's nearly over.'

'Call me Jenny,' Jenny suggested.

She blinked as she looked at the kitchen clock. It was nearly nine o'clock. By country standards, she had slept very late. She immediately felt guilty, and promised

26

herself to set her alarm in future. She didn't want to give Wayne Paterson any excuse to find her wanting in her duties, even if Bill Williams was her official employer.

'Wayne saddled the horses ages ago, and he's given you the old chestnut to ride,' Allan volunteered.

Jenny washed down her breakfast with a hasty mouthful of tea, rushed back into her room to grab her bathers, and then went outside. She stood a few seconds on the verandah looking around. Taralon was a pretty place, with just enough bush around to give the grounds a park like appearance.

The horses were tethered by the verandah. Jenny's mouth quirked up in a ready grin as she studied the solid chestnut mare with its high jumping saddle. Wayne was taking every precaution against her taking a fall from the horse! John was swinging on to a shaggy raw boned pony with its eyes nearly obscured by the heavy forelock. A resigned Shetland braced itself for Merry to clamber up, and Allan waited on a heavy looking mare with placid eyes, and leading a packhorse.

'I'm leading, 'cause I have to show you everything around the property,' he explained.

Jenny swung into the saddle of the chestnut mare with the first feeling of real pleasure she had experienced for a long time. The sky was blue, and the sun warm, and there was a spacious untrammelled feeling about the countryside.

'Wayne guessed the stirrups,' John volunteered. 'Do you need them adjusted?'

Jenny shook her head. They set off, with Merry trailing behind. Jenny's first day of duty had started. This morning the children looked more wary than hostile. Merry seemed the first to relax when she admired the lambs, and then John gradually got more talkative as he showed her the most important things around the property.

Allan made them all detour to have a look at the new season's foals, and Jenny nodded earnestly as John talked of their bloodlines.

They skirted the big back paddock and Jenny admired the new bull.

'Dad paid $17,000 for him,' John volunteered.

'Your Dad must have had a good season,' Jenny commented, suddenly aware of the lush pasture, and the healthy coats of the grazing cattle.

For a fleeting second John looked anxious and a lot older than his almost twelve years old. 'Yeah,' he said slowly.

'But I still haven't got my new saddle,' Allan grumbled.

'Your old one is all right for jumping, and don't start nagging Dad again or I'll thump you.'

Jenny hastily intervened.

'Are we going somewhere we can swim for our picnic? Mrs Harris reminded me to put in my bathers.'

John volunteered the information they had a special swimming spot at the river, and Wayne had put up a new rope to swing on. Allan's silence remained sullen.

The narrow track wound over the hill, and they closed the last gate on the boundary of Taralon. The denser bush closed around them. They rode in silence, broken by Merry's shrill requests for them to wait all the time. The small shabby Shetland pony walked slower and slower, as he showed his disapproval of their excursion away from the comfort of his home paddock.

Eventually, John got annoyed. He swung down, threw his reins over to Allan to hold, and tossed Merry up behind Allan, and mounted the Shetland.

'Giddup you brute,' he snapped.

The Shetland rolled his eyes, and recognising the firm hand, put his head down and broke into a frantic gallop past them to vanish up the track.

'Plays up on Merry,' Allan sniffed, as the shaggy pony vanished around the bend. 'He'll behave himself for a while.'

Much to Jenny's amusement they cantered on after the Shetland, Merry clinging unconcernedly to Allan's back.

When they caught up, and John lifted Merry back on to the small pony, the Shetland trotted meekly along beside them.

They made better time down the winding track which led beside the river, Jenny concentrated on pushing her chestnut mare along. It was almost as sluggish as the Shetland if she didn't keep it moving. She sensed the boys' approval as they watched her battle with the sluggish mare, and decided she had perhaps won through their wary reserve when John gave a satisfied nod.

It was nearing noon before the horses broke through into a clearing. The river curved around in a wide slow bend, and a rocky outcrop protected a shallow patch with clean sand edging the bank.

'We swim here when it's hot enough,' Merry bragged.

'Except you can't swim yet,' Allan jeered.

The horses made for the shade of the big gum, and the two boys unloaded the pack horse in a businesslike manner. Jenny swung down with a sigh of relief. It was months since she had ridden, and unaccustomed muscles protested.

Merry bustled around collecting twigs for the fire Allan was lighting. Soon a lazy curl of smoke came up, and John filled the billy at the water's edge. Jenny unsaddled the horses, and spread one of the rugs as a picnic rug.

'You know about horses, Miss Fleming?' John asked.

'Jenny,' she corrected. 'I used to spend my holidays with an uncle who had a property when I was a kid.'

There was a gradual lessening of the wariness. They nodded when she apologised that her uncle only ran sheep, but he always had horses, and she liked horses. By this time everything was ready, the sausages sizzling in the pan, and the billy boiling.

Jenny relaxed with a sigh of pleasure. It was a long time since she had tasted billy tea, and sausages so nicely fried in the blackened pan. This was a lot better than being huddled over the endless figures in the musty accountant's office at her last job.

After they had eaten, and Jenny promised Merry she could have her first swimming lesson as soon as her lunch had settled and after her afternoon nap, the two boys set up their fishing rods and sorted out their bait. The angling rods had been Christmas presents, John explained. Suddenly, Allan flared up again.

'But Dad promised me the new saddle,' he burst out. 'He's broken his word.'

'Ungrateful pig,' John yelled back and cuffed him.

Picnic mugs and plates scattered as the two boys flew at each other punching and kicking. Allan was smaller than John, but had a fiery temper that matched his hair. Jenny held the boys apart with difficulty. These sort of problems never rose in the office of Alltwine and Witfords.

'I'm ashamed of you two,' she scolded. 'Brothers should stick together, not fight.'

'He's got no right to nag Dad,' John ground out.

'And Dad's got no right to break his promise,' Allan retorted.

'It's none of Jenny's business,' John warned.

'He's had a good season,' Allan flung back, but he sneaked a worried look at Jenny as he picked up his rod, and lapsed into his silence again.

The boys and their rods disappeared upstream around the first bend past where the water rippled and frothed over the rocks. Jenny collected, washed and packed away the picnic things. She looked at the saddle she had taken from Allan's horse. It was an old stock saddle, polished up and in good condition. It was quite suitable for jumping with its high curved back and high pommel. Allan didn't look like a spoilt child, but he certainly sounded it.

The horses dozed under the tree, swishing their tails at the flies. Merry's breathing became regular as she fell asleep on the rug. Jenny looked at her book, and yawned. She leaned back and contemplated the ripples of the water, and the way the reflection of the trees shimmered and moved in the water.

Suddenly, the clearing seemed very quiet and isolated. She tensed. An extra shimmer of reflection among the trees looked like furtive movement. She scanned the opposite river bank. The trees and bushes lined it thickly. For a few seconds she thought she glimpsed something moving. She sat and watched until her eyes ached with the strain, but nothing moved.

She reached for her book, and continued reading. It was hard to shake the feeling unseen eyes were watching her. Several times, she lifted her eyes from her page and looked across at the other bank, but there was nothing to see.

She glanced across at the horses. They were alert and edgy, with their heads up snuffing the air, and ears forward. Suddenly, Jenny stopped enjoying her quiet picnic by the river. The deserted river bank seemed sinister and dangerous, despite the bright afternoon sunlight. The sense of being watched grew stronger.

The afternoon wore on. Merry slept and Jenny hiding her unease tried to keep reading. She greeted the return of the anglers with relief. They were glum faced and empty handed.

The decision was made to have a quick swim. They all changed into their bathers, and Jenny checking the bend was shallow, gave Merry her first swimming lesson, while the boys whooped and swung from the rope into the centre of the river, their earlier disagreement put behind them. Jenny watched them closely, but even Allan seemed to be a totally confident swimmer, so she concentrated on teaching Merry to float.

After a while, the decision that perhaps the water was still a bit too cold for too long a swim became a mutual one. They came out, dried and dressed. Merry was very excited about her progress in swimming, and her earlier wariness was forgotten as she chattered to Jenny about her next lesson.

They saddled up and set off at a brisk trot, Merry's little Shetland leading the way. Jenny heard the boys laugh out loud for the first time at the Shetland's eagerness to get home. Her own spontaneous chuckle rang out as well, but even as she laughed, Jenny looked over her shoulder for a last glimpse of their picnic spot.

She wasn't prepared to admit it, but secretly she was glad to be leaving the river, and the vague unease that had shadowed her the whole afternoon, lifted as they got further away from the river and closer to Taralon.

CHAPTER 3

The lights of the big house glowed through the dusk, and the horses quickened into a headlong gallop to reach the verandah. Jenny dismounted rather stiffly. A long red sports car was parked beside the big grey car.

'Tony and Marise are here again,' John grumbled.

Jenny looked at the disgust on both boys' faces. Why did the boys dislike Marise and her brother? Surely they should accept Marise if she had been working at the property for so long.

'I'm not going inside then,' Allan grumbled. 'I'll give you a hand with the horses.'

'You should go in. Wayne will want to know we got back safely,' John suggested, as Jenny prepared to follow them. 'Merry will be okay with us.'

'I'm supposed to be looking after you,' Jenny said doubtfully.

'We can look after ourselves,' John said tersely. 'We're used to it!'

Jenny hesitated, but the boys had already turned to lead the horses away, Merry still sitting on her small pony. The children had closed ranks at the sight of the red sports car, and once more their faces were hostile and wary. She decided it was the wrong time to push herself with them, so walked up the steps of the verandah.

She hesitated at the top of the steps, but Wayne called to her through the open French doors. She went into the brightly lit loungeroom. The stooped figure of her employer stood with his back to the fireplace. The wedding photo with the smiling black-haired bride and the sandy-haired groom with his merry blue eyes, was behind him on the mantelpiece.

Jenny was shocked to realise how much Bill Williams must have aged since the death of his wife. His hands shook as they held his glass. Grief had stripped every vestige of the young man of the wedding photo away. His eyes were the same washed out grey as his skin and hair, and gazed indifferently ahead of him. He gave Jenny a bewildered nod as she paused inside the door, as if he didn't remember who she was.

'The boys and Merry are unsaddling the horses, and will be along later. They said they didn't need any help,' Jenny explained to the room at large.

'You have met Marise and Tony Bickerton,' Wayne said. He was lounging back on the couch beside Marise.

'Of course,' Jenny agreed.

Looking at Marise, Jenny immediately felt untidy and dishevelled. The ride back had caused her hair to cascade untidily down her back in tangled curls, and she was aware her face was innocent of any makeup, and her shirt hanging out over her slacks. The original impression of Marise and her shining perfection was intensified at this second meeting. Marise wore a severe red silk blouse and grey tailored culottes, and despite the white cast on her leg, she managed to look elegant and at ease.

'It's nice to see a new face,' Tony rose from his chair as he spoke. He also had an elegant gloss to him, from his shining blonde hair, smooth tanned skin and the flashing white of his smile. There was open admiration in his eyes as he looked down at her. In contrast to his sister, he radiated friendliness and good humour. 'Would you like a drink, Jenny?'

'Make it a lemon squash,' Wayne suggested.

'A small cream sherry, thank you,' Jenny said, unaccountably irritated at the too smooth suggestion from Wayne. She gave Tony her trusting wide smile. How dare Wayne try to dictate what she drank, as if she was a child!

Tony obediently brought across the small glass of sherry, and put a friendly arm across her shoulders as he steered her towards a two-seater lounge. 'Come and tell me all about yourself,' he coaxed. 'You don't look old enough to be allowed out without a keeper, much less be able to hold down a job which kept Marise flat out.'

Marise's chuckle was malicious. 'Don't get your head turned by Tony, little Jenny Wren, even if a new face is a novelty.'

Jenny managed a polite smile. The smile on Tony's face faded, and his hazel eyes went hard. He gave his sister a smouldering stare, but she had turned her back on him to murmur something in an intimate manner to Wayne.

'The boys took you for a picnic did they?' Tony asked. 'What do you think of the countryside?'

His arm was still draped casually across her shoulders in an almost proprietary manner. Jenny tried to ignore it. Tony seemed a naturally friendly person, and there was no way she could ease away from him on the small couch without drawing attention to her action.

'We ended up at a place called Panniken Bend,' she explained. 'The water was a bit cold, but we all went swimming. The boys played on the rope, and Merry had her first swimming lesson. The boys seem quite confident in the water though. I guess they have had plenty of practice swimming.'

For a fraction of a second, Tony's pleasant expression faded, leaving a suspicious shadow on his face. 'Panniken Bend,' he said slowly. 'Not a very safe place. The river is still deep in places and treacherous. There are less dangerous places to swim for a newcomer to the district.'

Jenny hesitated. It was on the tip of her tongue to make a passing allusion to the sense of being watched at Panniken Bend. There was an odd pause. She had the impression that Wayne was suddenly tense and listening carefully. Marise had turned her head and watched her too, a curious glint in her hazel eyes.

Jenny plunged into conversation again. 'I would have supposed there would have been a lot more water around. By the look of the property, it's been a good winter for rain.'

'Yes, we have all had quite a good season,' Wayne said in a dry voice.

Bill Williams scowled, and lines of worry and anxiety deepened on his face. 'A very good season,' he echoed hollowly.

Jenny flushed, and wondered desperately what she had said wrong, to bring such an odd mood to the assembled company. The look in Marise's eyes was calculating, and her brother looked uncomfortable.

'The boys spent the afternoon fishing, without success,' she almost gabbled. 'Are there really any fish in the river?'

The atmosphere lightened, and the conversation turned to fishing, and the respective merits of various flies and correct bait. Then the conversation turned back to horses, and the forthcoming race meeting. Jenny was surprised to learn that the Bickertons and Bill Williams had entered horses in the race meeting.

'Black Prince is coming along nicely,' Tony

bragged cheerfully. 'He is going to give Pretty Boy a run for his money this year.'

Bill Williams roused himself to speak. 'I don't know,' he said doubtfully. 'Gwenda thought...' his voice tailed off, and the bewildered look returned to his eyes.

'Gwenda has done a magnificent job of getting Pretty Boy ready for the meeting,' Wayne said heartily, too heartily Jenny thought. 'Of course Gwenda expected Pretty Boy to beat Black Prince at the next meeting.'

'Gwenda worked very hard to bring Pretty Boy up to form,' the older man said with a semblance of pride, and then he lapsed into silence, and the light died out of his eyes again. At that moment, Mrs Harris entered the room. She nodded to Bill Williams, but addressed herself to Wayne.

'Dinner is nearly ready, and are Marise and Tony staying?'

Marise exchanged a glance with Tony. Some decision was arrived at. 'Thanks for the invite, but we really have to get back,'

Marise said. She put a firm hand on Wayne's arm. 'Help me up, Wayne.'

Mrs Harris left the room. Marise collected her crutches and managed to stand up, swaying against Wayne; a tall girl with shining fair hair, and an inviting curve to her red lips. She swung across the room with Wayne beside her. The stooped man by the mantelpiece didn't move, his faded eyes still gazing into space. Wayne opened the French doors and there was a low intimate chuckle from Marise as he picked her up and carried her down the steps.

Tony dropped his arm around Jenny's waist and pulled her against him, ignoring the absent gaze of his host.

'There are a lot more interesting places to visit around the district than Panniken Bend,' he said easily. His head was so close to Jenny that she could smell the whisky on his breath. 'What about it, Jenny Wren? I'd like to show you around.'

'When I have some spare time, perhaps,' Jenny said, keeping the smile on her lips with an effort.

She started to feel uncomfortable. Tony was still smiling, but his hazel eyes had hardened at her evasive answer. He really was holding her much too tightly against him for a casual acquaintance. She glanced at her employer, but he didn't appear to notice them. Tony lowered his head even closer so that his lips brushed hers. She tried to pull back, but the arm around her waist was iron hard.

'We're sure to have a lot in common,' he murmured. 'So don't keep me waiting too long, little Jenny.'

There was almost a veiled warning in his voice. Jenny stiffened against the pressure of his arm. She decided that it might not be a good idea to give the over-friendly Tony any encouragement. He was reading too much into her determination to be polite. Before she could say anything however, Wayne had returned and spoke, his voice dry.

'At the moment you're keeping Marise waiting.'

Tony uncurled himself from beside Jenny, and the crushing pressure of his arm around her waist was gone. She took the opportunity to stand up, realising to her fury that her face was flaming as red as a guilty schoolgirl's, although she had done nothing to feel guilty about.

'And Marise lacks patience to wait too long,' Tony agreed cheerfully. He waved a casual hand at Jenny. 'Don't forget that I have first claim on your time when you have some to spare,' he said with his flashing smile, and then disappeared down the verandah steps with Wayne beside him.

Jenny heard the murmur of voices, then the roar of the sports car accelerating into life, and the noise of the car faded into the distance. Wayne's footsteps marched briskly across the verandah and into the room. His brows were a straight black bar across his blazing grey eyes.

He grasped Jenny's arm in a painfully tight grip and propelled her out onto the verandah without saying anything. Her employer still stood against the mantel-piece. He had not farewelled his guests, and didn't seem to notice that Wayne had almost dragged Jenny out on to the verandah.

Although the light streamed out from the dining and kitchen windows, and in an even brighter bar from the open French windows of the loungeroom, the verandah itself was shadowy, and Wayne's face was a paler blur in the darkness. From the kitchen came the appetising smells of food cooking, and the clink of Mrs Harris setting up the big table in the dining room off the kitchen.

'While you are employed here, you will not get friendly with Tony Bickerton, and that is an order,' Wayne snapped.

'I really should check Merry. She is sure to need a bath before tea,' Jenny said, ignoring Wayne's odd outburst.

Much to her surprise, Wayne grasped her shoulders and shook her. 'You are a little fool, but I am warning you. Tony is not a suitable playmate for you!'

'Kindly remove your hands,' Jenny

stammered in rage. 'Do you realise that what you are doing constitutes assault and battery, and hardly correct behaviour? I believe that Bill Williams is my employer, not you, so mind your own business.'

Wayne released her so unexpectedly, she staggered. She could hear his heavy breathing. He was a dark bulk towering over her, and she took a step back from him.

'As I was silly enough to bring you up here, you are my responsibility and my business,' he ground out.

'What I do in my own time is my own business,' Jenny flashed back, forgetting her original distaste and distrust of Tony in her rage. 'I assume I am going to have some time of my own, in accordance with the usual custom of rostered time off for live-in employees.' He remained silent. 'Or do you have a waiting cell with a chain with my name on it for my rostered day off?'

'Don't be ridiculous,' Wayne drawled. Jenny realised his rage was icy. 'Just remember what I said. You are our responsibility while you are employed at Taralon.'

'I'm big enough to take responsibility for my own actions, thank you,' Jenny retorted. 'So spare me your feudal attitude.'

She slammed into the kitchen breathing hard. She hadn't lost her temper for years. She prided herself on her self control. Although she had to admit being physically manhandled by someone was certainly sufficient reason to blow her top. That arrogant man was trying to treat her as if she wasn't any older than Merry, throwing his weight around as if he owned her. She was going to have to stamp on his toes hard to stop him from getting too high-handed. She should have known she raged to herself, that Wayne Paterson was going to be the one unpleasantness in her stay at this pleasant property.

'I've already put Merry into the bath, and don't worry about the boys. Wayne always supervises their showers,' Mrs Harris said cheerfully, as she came back into the kitchen. She looked at Jenny more closely. 'You certainly have got a touch of the sun today, my dear. Your face looks quite red.'

'Yes,' Jenny said inadequately, and fled to supervise Merry's bathtime.

One way or the other, her first day at Taralon had managed to prove quite eventful.

CHAPTER 4

Jenny nibbled at the pen, and turned over a new page on the ledger. The door of the small office was open, and the sun streamed through like a solid yellow block. It was still too early for the sun to move around to filter through the tangled wisteria along the verandah. She thought about shutting the door, but decided that the heat was pleasant rather than uncomfortable. Although it made her feel sleepy and the figures in front of her hard to concentrate on.

She had been at Taralon for a whole week. Her life had settled into a pleasant routine. After breakfast the boys yelled their farewells as their father drove them off to meet the school bus. She and Merry then retired to the small cluttered office off the verandah. Merry sat at her own little desk, and scribbled on spare sheets of paper, until Jenny finished the bookwork. When she finished it was time for the excursion around the property to inspect all the baby animals. After lunch Merry was borne off by Mrs Harris for her afternoon nap, and Jenny had a few hours to herself. Sometimes she went for a walk or saddled a horse and rode, and sometimes relaxed on the shady verandah with a book.

The back of Jenny's neck prickled, and she lifted her head, aware of her visitor even before Merry's delighted squeal of 'Hi, Uncle Wayne,' as she flung herself at him.

Wayne Paterson caught Merry and threw her into the air, and then waited with her cuddled into his arms. Jenny gave him a distant nod. To her embarrassment, she felt her cheeks flush hotly.

She was unsure of where she stood with him. She had not seen him to talk to since their argument of the previous week. One of the hands had mentioned he had been supervising the excavation of the new dam at the other end of the property, but the fact he had not the decency to seek her out to apologise still rankled.

The amusement died out of his eyes as he returned her look. Tiredness and strain were plain on his face, and his brows drew across in their forbidding bar. Jenny knew that he put long hours and hard work into the management of Taralon, but then he countersigned the cheques so he obviously had a financial interest in the place. Bill Williams still drifted around like a grey ineffectual ghost, leaving the decision making and any practical work to his brother-in-law.

'I don't want to interrupt two hard working ladies,' Wayne said smoothly. 'Where's Bill?'

'He's down at the stables,' Jenny said with equal courtesy. 'He's worried about Pretty Boy.'

Wayne put Merry down without a word, and departed. Jenny watched his progress towards the stables. He moved very quietly for a big man, yet he gave off an aura of suppressed energy and power that was so tangible that Jenny had to admit she could sense his presence before she even saw him.

'Uncle Wayne cross,' Merry remarked as she returned to her jumble of crisscross lines on her paper.

Jenny ignored her, and sat pen in hand. Mrs Harris had been in a talkative mood one morning when Jenny was helping with the jam making.

'I never thought Wayne would be such a hard man,' she had sighed. 'He's not grieving like poor Bill, and yet he and Gwenda were so close.'

'Some people hide their grief,' Jenny ventured, suddenly remembering the anguish she had glimpsed on his face when he had talked of his sister's death.

'Of course, Bill's lucky he's willing to pitch in,' Mrs Harris rambled on. 'He's supposed to be a silent partner, but he hardly has time to eat between being here and trying to keep an eye on his own place.'

Jenny continued cutting up fruit, and remained silent, but Mrs Harris was in full spate. So she heard all about Wayne Paterson's success in building up a herd of good quality cattle, and his innovative ideas on cattle breeding, stocking and land management.

'He's renovated the cottage on Paterley,' Mrs Harris mused aloud. 'I believe it looks lovely. We're all wondering if he's got the idea of marrying. He and Marise have got very friendly.'

'They seem well suited,' Jenny agreed in a colourless voice.

'I wouldn't say that,' Mrs Harris sniffed. 'Spoilt! She and her brother both, with all those fancy overseas schools, and extravagant ideas. Wayne could do better.'

Jenny turned the conversation back to the practicalities of whether the first lot of jam had been boiling long enough to jell. She didn't want to listen to gossip, but Mrs Harris was in a chatty mood.

Jenny then heard all about the Bickertons,

their lavish entertaining, their overseas trips and their expensive cars. The twins had been running their property since the death of their parents in a plane crash.

'Of course Tony runs their place very successfully,' Mrs Harris's praise was grudging. 'He'd have to to afford their expensive tastes. It was his idea that Marise help Gwenda. I don't know why Gwenda became so influenced by her? She's got a nasty tongue.' Marise did have a nasty tongue, Jenny agreed to herself. She understood why the children didn't like her. Even Merry's sunny face shadowed when she came around.

She sighed, and returned to copying figures. Maybe it wasn't Marise and her antagonism and nasty tongue, but somehow there seemed to be a blight on the place that made her vaguely uncomfortable. The tragic death of Gwenda Williams was shocking, but surely the tension and strain on the faces around her should be easing as they accepted the grim fact of her death.

Jenny's eyes studied the neat column of figures. All the well covered cattle were bringing good market prices this season. Yet, despite the good season, a lot of the neighbours who dropped in had the same expressions of gloom and worry on their faces.

She was glad that her position was only temporary. Taralon was a pretty place basking in its pleasant sunlit valley, and under normal circumstances, excluding the feudal attitude of Wayne Paterson, she would have loved working here. The three young hands always gave her shy but pleased grins as they passed; Mrs Harris was a darling, and she was already very attached to Merry, and genuinely liked the two boys and their gentle absent father, yet although she didn't consider herself sensitive to atmosphere, there was an inexplicable tension over the place.

She shut the ledger with a snap. She was too unsettled to concentrate on figures. Merry had left, but her high pitched voice could be heard from the kitchen. Jenny went to investigate. Mrs Harris was cooking, and looked flustered as Merry grabbed a scrap of pastry. Relief swept over her face at the sight of Jenny.

'I'll cook your gingerbread man, Merry,' she coaxed. 'You and Jenny go down and visit Pretty Boy until lunch is ready.'

Merry's flushed face was sulky. 'I don't want to see Pretty Boy. I want to help.'

'Your Uncle Wayne might be down there,' Mrs Harris coaxed.

Merry's face lit up as she remembered that her Uncle Wayne would indeed be down at the stables. She ran out the door immediately. Jenny managed a smile for Mrs Harris as she followed her out. The stables were the last place she wanted to be if Wayne was there, but keeping an eye on Merry was part of her morning duties.

Pretty Boy was in the small yard beside the stables. He stood placidly, his chestnut coat glowing in the sun. The two men leaned against him talking quietly. They stopped talking and waited in silence as Merry, with Jenny following approached. Wayne swung Merry up, and sat her on the fence.

'Pretty Boy doesn't look very sick,' Jenny commented. Pretty Boy put his ears forward and whinnied a welcome. Jenny had been a frequent visitor in her leisure time, and he nudged at her pocket for his expected titbit. She fed him one lump of sugar. 'Why the worried faces?'

Bill Williams gave a sudden smile, and the worried lines on his face eased.

'He's pulled a tendon,' he explained. 'But it is only six weeks to the race meeting.'

For a few seconds, he looked almost normal, his eyes keen and his face years younger. Jenny suspected that his concern for the horse Pretty Boy, his dead wife's passion and hobby, was taking his mind off his grief.

'He looks fit enough to me to win the race with both back legs hobbled,' Jenny ventured with a smile.

'A loyal statement from an admirer of

Pretty Boy,' Wayne teased, smiling down at her. 'But we will put our hopes on him winning without that sort of handicap.'

'And your money too,' Jenny said primly, trying to keep her eyes from dancing her amusement.

She suddenly felt light-hearted, as if the intangible blight over her was removed. She would never forgive nor forget Wayne's boorish treatment of her the previous week she told herself, but it was easy to understand his popularity when he concentrated his teasing smile on her.

It was a smile that transformed his entire face, and he looked a different person. The smiles he gave Merry, or Mrs Harris or even Marise weren't like this one. His black brows arched, and his face was suddenly younger and alive with mirth. His grey eyes softened as they crinkled up, with an understanding twinkle in them. Something deep inside Jenny responded, despite herself. She could feel the warmth of her smile which idiotically refused to fade.

'You will come to see him race with the rest of us?' Bill demanded still with the relaxed expression on his face, as he leaned against the horse.

'That sounds like fun,' Jenny agreed.

'The whole district gathers for the meeting,' Wayne explained, still with that smile on his face. 'And for the dinner party afterwards and the ball.'

'I'm coming too,' Merry said excitedly.

'For the afternoon only, young lady,' Wayne warned. He glanced back at his brother-in-law. 'What about staying for the rest of the racing carnival like you usually do?'

The light died out of Bill Williams's eyes, and the absent grey look closed down over his face. Whatever memories he had of the rest of the racing carnival were suddenly bleak and unpleasant.

'Pretty Boy is racing on the Saturday, so I'll return with him straight after the race.'

'You have to stay for the celebration dinner when Pretty Boy wins,' Wayne urged.

He was almost looking anxious. He gave Jenny an odd look of appeal. 'And all your employees will stay for the ball. It's the custom!'

'I certainly would love to meet all your neighbours and stay for the ball,' Jenny pleaded with a smile. 'If I'm allowed to come, that is?'

'Of course,' her employer assured her, suddenly recollecting his manners. 'I suppose it would be selfish of me to spoil everyone's day out by leaving early.' This earned Jenny a quick glance of gratitude from Wayne which was so warming she could feel the heat in her pinkening cheeks. Bill's faded eyes focused on her. 'Life is quiet enough around here for a pretty young girl like yourself.'

'Never,' Jenny contradicted eagerly. 'I just love being here. There's always lots of things happening.'

The silence lengthened and lengthened. The two men exchanged grim looks. Jenny tried to keep the smile on her mouth, but it felt forced. What had she said wrong this time?

'I want to go back to the house,' Merry pouted, breaking the silence. 'Mrs Harris is cooking my gingerbread man.'

'Morning tea sounds a good idea,' Wayne agreed as he lifted her down from the fence. 'I heard about Mrs Harris making gingerbread men.'

'And I made one specially for you,' Merry called back as she ran on ahead.

The three adults walked back to the house. The strained grey absent look was back on Bill Williams's face. Wayne's brows had lowered in their forbidding bar, and he looked morose and preoccupied.

Jenny didn't try to break the silence. Her earlier light-hearted merriment had evaporated completely. Why had she forgotten Wayne's unpleasant feudal streak so easily to warm to his charm anyway? What had she said to offend?

She was only trying to reassure her employer when she babbled that there were lots of things happening at Taralon! Why had her innocent remark caused the atmosphere of the pleasant morning to change so quickly? Despite the hot sun, she shivered, as she sensed the intangible brooding tension of Taralon back over her.

CHAPTER 5

Her free time after lunch was the nicest time of the day, Jenny decided. She was settled on the verandah with a book, the sun filtering warm through the tangled wisteria. Taralon seemed to sleep in the noonday warmth and the only sound was the drowsy hum of bees in the purple flowers.

She listened with half an ear as the discussion about Pretty Boy went on and on. The two men had settled on the verandah to finish their tea, and Bill was roused out of his apathy to argue the merits of the elderly veterinarian who had been so helpful about the strained tendon. Jenny, trying to concentrate on her book, got the impression that Wayne was taking the opposite view just to get him talking.

The hum of voices stopped suddenly.

Jenny looked up from her book. Tony Bickerton had arrived. He was dressed casually in jeans and a check shirt. Bill gave him a vague smile, and Wayne the slightest of nods. With his arrival, the pleasant relaxed atmosphere was suddenly gone. Tony gave them a flashing smile, but addressed himself to Jenny.

'You promised to come riding, Jenny Wren. I see you've forgotten!'

Jenny flushed. She had evaded Tony's insistent invitations when he called by saying she didn't know when she had any free time. She looked across at the showy chestnut horse tied to the rails. Tony had now made it look as if she had arranged to go with him without consulting her employer.

She opened her mouth to come out with a polite refusal and an apology, deciding again that Tony Bickerton had encroaching ways when he wasn't checked. It was the very stillness of posture that alerted her to Wayne. His face was expressionless, the grey eyes under the straight bars of brows like icy chips. She sensed he was furious.

She stared at him in silent defiance. So he was furious? His smiling charm of the morning had almost obscured the memory of his weird feudal attitude, an attitude that was completely inexplicable. It was no business of his who she went out with and where? He had no right to dictate her actions! She listened to herself answer recklessly.

'If it's all right with Bill and Mrs Harris, I'd love to come riding with you.'

'A break will do you good,' Mrs Harris agreed. She must have seen Tony ride up, and stood smiling by the kitchen door. 'Wayne can saddle a horse. You go and get changed.'

Tony's smile flashed even brighter. Wayne stood up without a word. Jenny fled inside to change into jeans. When she returned, Buttercup had been saddled and waited by the chestnut horse at the rail, and Wayne and her employer had gone.

'We can ride over to our place and have a look at Dark Prince,' Tony suggested, as he got back on his horse after closing Taralon's last gate behind them. 'We can cut cross country.'

They set off, and Tony reined back his horse to keep pace with the stolid Buttercup. Tony was on his best behaviour, polite and informative. The sun was warm and the air fresh, and Jenny's spirits rose. Tony seemed a different person away from his sister. He pointed out the boundary of their property, which curved alongside the river.

'It's bigger than Taralon, but only the plains along the river are any good for grazing,' he explained. 'Like Taralon we run mainly beef cattle. Our great grandfather called the property Millalong.' He gave a short laugh. 'Marise and I thought it a very suitable name when we discovered what a mess we had inherited.'

'Was there a mill here originally?'

'Not even a trace left now,' Tony said more

cheerfully. 'The old boy built it above the falls. We will have a picnic there one day.'

'Perhaps,' Jenny agreed.

Her pleasure at her outing dimmed when she arrived at the homestead. It was a beautiful and gracious building, and reared in all its elegant grandeur in a very English style garden. There was certainly nothing homely or comfortable or for that matter, welcoming about it. Marise swung out on her crutches to invite her in, but hardly bothered to conceal her annoyance and dislike. Tony's face darkened at his reception. Jenny forced down a drink of tea and some cake in the aloof high ceilinged drawing room, and reminded him he was going to show her Black Prince.

Tony looked relieved, and whisked her out to admire the horse. Jenny was able to say with perfect truth that Black Prince was the most magnificent horse she had ever seen. However, she had no desire to see him from a closer viewpoint than the high wooden rail. He lacked Pretty Boy's spoiled docility and friendliness. As soon as he saw them, he flung his head back, his nostrils flaring and his eyes rolling, and edged away from them, muscles rippling under his shining black coat.

'He's quite mad,' Tony said proudly. 'But pointed in the right direction he's faster than anything else on four legs.'

'I can understand your confidence in him,' Jenny agreed as they returned along the track that led off the property. 'He looks unbeatable.'

She was relieved they had left Millalong. It was run efficiently and in meticulous order, but the aura it radiated was a hostile one. The hands were sullen faced and morose, and the elderly woman who acted as housekeeper and cook was equally wary and disdainful as she had shuffled in with the afternoon tea tray.

'What about coming down the river for a quick swim,' Tony suggested. 'It's warm enough, and I know a much better spot than Panniken Bend.'

'It's getting late, and I have to get back. Mrs Harris is short handed this afternoon.' Jenny said coolly. She wondered if Tony expected her to go skinny dipping? There had been no suggestion that she bring bathers or a towel with her.

'That's her problem,' Tony said sullenly. He sneaked a sidelong glance at her. 'Are you using her as an excuse to avoid me, Jenny Wren?'

'Don't be ridiculous.'

Tony was silent until they reached the top of the hill. From here could be seen most of Taralon and the Millalong property, with the river edging a natural boundary beside them. Tony dismounted, and reached for Jenny to lift her down.

'I want to get to know you a lot better,' he murmured, without releasing her from his arms. 'You should be more friendly,' he continued into her stiff silence as he dropped a light kiss on her mouth.

'I'm friendly enough,' Jenny answered lightly, and stepped back under the pretence of soothing Buttercup.

'I think you'll find it easier to become a lot friendlier, Jenny Wren,' he coaxed. He looked down at Taralon, shimmering in the sleepy haze of the afternoon heat. 'You don't belong in a backward dump like this. I'll show you a good time when Dark Prince wins.'

'Counting your chickens before they hatch,' Jenny teased. 'Dark Prince still has to beat Pretty Boy, and the other seven starters.' Tony's face darkened. For a few seconds Jenny was shocked at the reckless, bitter and desperate expression his face wore. She changed the subject. 'It's been a lovely break, but I really do have to get back.'

Tony helped her up into the saddle, and put a restraining hand on the bridle. 'I'll see you again,' he insisted.

'Of course,' Jenny agreed.

Buttercup, sensing her unease, tossed his head and fidgeted until she loosened the reins and she headed home to Taralon at her fast trot. She sensed Tony's brooding gaze until she had turned into the shelter of the trees along the winding driveway.

To extend a light-hearted friendship to him was one thing, to cope with his unpredictable intensity and demands for an instant relationship was another. Despite the flashing smile and friendliness, she sensed he was as unstable as Black Prince, with hidden depths of bitterness and resentment. The thought crossed her mind, to be suppressed almost at once, that perhaps Wayne Paterson had a logical reason for forbidding a closer acquaintance.

When she eventually got back, unsaddled and rubbed down Buttercup, the boys were home from school, and playing a noisy game of football. There was no sign of the grey Mercedes, and she asked no questions when Wayne didn't join them for dinner.

After bathing and bedding down Merry, and supervising the boys' inevitable homework, she relaxed in the lounge. Mrs Harris placidly knitted in front of the television.

Bill Williams just sat, as was his usual custom, staring at nothing. When the subject of Merry's clothes came up, Jenny volunteered to finish her party dress.

'Gwenda was making it for her fifth birthday,' Mrs Harris explained. The knitting needles slowed for a few seconds. 'It's been in the sewing basket, since...'

'I quite like hand sewing,' Jenny said hastily.

It was a pink velvet dress with lace around the collar. Jenny found the needle and cotton and started to tack up the ruffled hem. She sewed until Mrs Harris yawned and went to bed. After a while Bill Williams stirred himself, and looked at his watch.

'Don't sit up half the night with that, Jenny,' he said in his absent manner. 'It's getting late.'

'I won't be much longer,' Jenny promised. 'Just a few buttons to sew on.'

He left the room. Jenny turned off the television and the overhead light, and sewed by the light of the small shaded lamp. After she had sewed the buttons on, she had to make the buttonholes. It was tedious and time consuming, and she finished the last one with a sigh of relief.

She stood up and stretched. Everything was very quiet. It was nearly one o'clock in the morning. She turned the light off, and walked over to the French windows.

The bright moonlight lit the property, every fence and roof distinct, the large gums throwing deep pools of shadow across the yard and stables. A light flashed for a brief second behind the furthermost group of buildings. Jenny blinked and looked again. That particular building was used to store harnesses and spare saddles and rusting farm machinery. Just beside it were the stables.

Who could be prowling around at this hour? Perhaps one of the animals was sick? She stepped through the French windows, and walked quietly along the verandah down the steps, and along the side track that led to the furthermost buildings. She pushed past the large flowering shrub at the end of the stables, and worked her way around the back against the barred fence.

From behind, an arm went roughly around her waist, and a hand clamped across her mouth. She tried to scream, and bit savagely. There was a muffled curse as she was lifted off her feet and dragged into the shadows.

'Quiet Jenny,' whispered her employer's voice.

The arm around her waist relaxed, and she was put down again. She made out the white blur of Bill Williams's face. He wore a dark high necked sweater, and leaned against a tree, rifle under his arm. She turned around. Her attacker, Wayne Paterson was examining his hand where she had bit him.

'What are you doing at this hour of night?' she whispered.

'Later,' Wayne whispered back.

Through the darkness could be heard the muffled noise of a motor. It seemed to be coming towards them across the paddock. The dark bulk of a truck appeared. It had no lights on. In one fluid motion Wayne picked up a rifle. Jenny widened her eyes. What was going on? Who was driving the truck?

She tried to work out where the truck was coming from. The road was four paddocks away. To come from that direction they would have had to cut the fences to drive through.

The truck stopped. Dark figures jumped out the back, and let down the tail gate to make a ramp. Jenny drew her breath in with shock, as the figures moved towards the stables.

'All right,' Wayne warned, his voice loud and brisk. 'That's far enough – move away from the truck.'

He stepped out of the shadows with Bill Williams beside him, and the moonlight glinted on the rifles. The dark forms froze, and then everything happened at once.

A dark figure at the front of the truck

threw something. Wayne dropped without a sound, and Bill Williams fired before he went down under the attacking dark shadows.

Jenny screamed and screamed. The floodlights lit up the stable area. Three of the station hands came sprinting down the path. The truck motor revved loudly, and the shadows attacking Bill Williams fled for the truck.

The truck started to move, tail gate bumping behind it, and two figures chased it fleetly to scramble up into the back. Bill Williams sat up and grabbed for his rifle, and fired. The truck swerved and lurched, gathered speed, and bumped over the slight rise. There were no lights to show its passage across the paddocks. The sound of its engine died away.

'Everyone okay?' someone asked.

Bill Williams scrambled to his feet. Jenny dropped down beside the still body of Wayne.

'Missed them!' Bill Williams sounded

annoyed. 'Where the devil were you blokes? You were supposed to watch the southern boundary!'

The taller figure sounded apologetic. 'Sorry boss, but there was a car parked over by the long paddock and we waited there. The truck must have cut through along the creek.'

Jenny glanced up, her finger on the uneven pulse of Wayne's wrist. 'What's going on?'

'We'll get Wayne up to the house and have a look at him,' her employer said, sounding unusually brisk and practical.

The men stooped to pick him up. Jenny stopped them.

'Use one of the hurdles,' she directed.

Her employer nodded agreement, and with Wayne limp on the hurdle, the slow procession wound up to the house. Jenny sped down to the bathroom for the first aid kit. On her way back to Wayne's room she overheard the muttered orders of her employer.

'This time patrol nearer the stables. Are all

the cattle out of the creek paddocks?'

There were muttered acknowledgements, and figures slouched off through the darkness. Bill Williams ran his hand through his greying hair and sighed.

'Let's see how he is then,' he said.

Wayne's face was colourless, except for the large purple bruise on one temple. His breathing was heavy and loud.

'Could be concussion, if nothing worse,' Jenny decided as she bathed his temples. 'Have you called the doctor?'

'He's coming over.'

'What's going on?' Jenny insisted.

'Having a bit of trouble with rustlers,' he admitted.

'Rustlers,' Jenny echoed. 'I thought they went out with the Wild West.'

'The whole district has suffered,' Bill Williams explained. 'The worst of it is they seem to know where and when to make their raids. It's always the most valuable animals we lose. They cut the fences, push the animals into a truck and take off.' He prowled restlessly up and down the room. 'Can't put up a roadblock, and search every truck going through. The highway has a continual convoy of trucks, all loaded with cattle on their way to market.'

Jenny concentrated on bathing Wayne's forehead. Rustlers in the twentieth century! So this was the reason for the worry of the local property owners, despite their good year! This was why Allan wasn't getting his promised new saddle.

'It's always worse this time of the year. We've been patrolling the properties constantly for the last several weeks. I dunno why they were trying for Pretty Boy though?'

Wayne groaned, and his eyes flickered. Jenny brushed his hair back and felt his forehead. It was hot to touch. Wayne opened grey eyes and looked at Jenny.

'What did pretty Jenny Wren grow into – a parrot or a vulture,' he muttered. He started to thresh around.

'Delirious,' Bill Williams predicted gloomily.

It was a frightening few hours. Wayne raved and threshed and his temperature stayed alarmingly high. At one stage he vomited, and later he shivered with an uncontrollable cold, and they piled blankets over him. The doctor was tired and terse when he examined him. It was nearly dawn, and he had covered a distance of seventy kilometres.

'Concussion probably. Doesn't seem to be any fracture.' He closed his bag. 'Keep him quiet for a few days.'

'Like some coffee?' Bill Williams suggested.

The two men strolled from the room, and Jenny turned off the light, weak yellow in the strengthening daylight. She studied the sleeping figure on the bed. Wayne looked a lot younger and more vulnerable, and not at all like the grim bad tempered dictator of Taralon. The door opened again and Bill Williams tiptoed in with a mug of coffee.

'Come on, Jenny.' His tone was kind. 'You've had quite a night.'

Jenny gave him a grateful smile and drank the coffee. The first rays of the morning sun slanted into the room, and her stare was vacant as she watched the dust motes dance in the golden rays.

'Jenny,' Bill Williams said again.

Jenny blinked awake with a start, and with a last quick glance at the figure on the bed, walked down the long passage to her own room.

She undressed and tumbled into bed. Although she was tired, sleep was a while in coming. She wondered how she could have been so unaware of what was going on. She had taken a lot of things for granted; the new floodlights around the stables area; the hands sitting up with sick animals, and Bill Williams's horror when he discovered her out walking one night by herself.

'I'm stupid, that's what,' she scolded herself, and on that note of self accusation, fell into a nightmare filled sleep of bumping trucks and rifle shots in the dark.

CHAPTER 6

Jenny chewed her pen, looked down at her notepaper and sighed. Her weekly letter to her mother was getting harder and harder to write. There seemed to be so much she couldn't say.

'You would have been impressed with my sewing ability, as I actually finished Merry's party dress, buttonholes and all. Wayne Paterson taught John to play chess, while recuperating after an accident.'

Should she comment about how improved he was on closer acquaintance despite his feudal streak? Or was he just trying to be polite? Jenny took over the brunt of the nursing for the two days he was kept in bed. Bill Williams shook himself out of his apathy and vanished to take over the management of his own property.

Not that Wayne had been a difficult patient, she told herself hastily. He was quiet, appreciative of her efforts, and when he felt well enough to be bored with the enforced rest, he sprawled on the battered couch in the office. Jenny was surprised to realise she actually enjoyed his company. They discovered they had the same tastes in their reading and music, and liked animals and mystery novels.

She continued her letter. 'He has gone back to work, and now John is trying to teach Allan to play chess, and whoever thought chess was a quiet game hasn't heard them argue over moves.'

She looked at what she had written. Better not write that Wayne had kissed her this morning when he left. The incident took place in front of Merry, who jumped up and down and chanted, 'Uncle Wayne kissed you. Uncle Wayne kissed you.' Bill Williams, waiting at the bottom of the steps, had watched in amusement.

Jenny thought about that kiss again. It was

only a light brotherly kiss, just the merest butterfly touch on her lips, but despite her efforts, tell tale colour had flooded her face. Almost as if she had never ever been kissed before, she thought indignantly, staring defiantly up into his eyes. Her unexpected reaction had somehow transferred itself to her knees which had gone curiously bone-less. Wayne's eyes became a more intense grey, and he touched her hot cheek in the lightest of caresses.

Jenny couldn't make up her mind whether she was pleased or offended. It wasn't an offensive kiss, just a friendly one, but she had done nothing to encourage that sort of friendliness. It was embarrassing that the colour had surged up into her face so hotly at the touch of his mouth. He was probably conceited enough to think he had made an impression on her.

Which he had, jeered the unconvinced part of her mind. No one had caused her knees to feel so boneless before. If he had put his arms around her and kissed her properly, how would she have reacted. Jenny's face flamed again at the intrusive curiosity of her undisciplined mind. She decided to finish her letter, and reached over to address an envelope.

Merry had spent the morning preoccupied with playing nurse. A row of battered dolls all had fresh bandages around their heads and her crooning babble had gone on and on as she played. The crooning babble suddenly stopped. Merry looked up and realised that Marise watched them from the doorway.

'I'm sorry,' Jenny said. It was an effort to keep her tone pleasant, remembering Marise's unconcealed dislike of her. 'I didn't hear you knock!'

'I left the car around the back, and walked through the house,' Marise explained.

Today she had a smaller and less cumbersome cast about her ankle, and she was without crutches. She was obviously getting better fast. She was dressed in a white silk shirt, and well tailored culottes. Her hair flowed back in an immaculate chignon like polished gold silk. She looked older with her hair pulled back so severely. Her lips were narrowed into a tight unfriendly line, and there was a calculating look in her hazel eyes.

Jenny was immediately aware of how faded her tee shirt was, and that her jeans were crumpled. She brushed back her hair which had tumbled around her shoulders as she had worked. Marise always made her feel about the same age as Merry.

'The place seems very quiet. Where is everybody?' Marise drawled.

Jenny stood up and walked out to the verandah. Merry unnoticed made a subdued escape. It was probably her insolent tone which got her hackles up Jenny decided. She kept the pleasant expression on her face with an effort of will. Why did Marise so obviously consider her an usurper? After all, she was only here on a temporary basis. Marise would be returning to Taralon as soon as her leg was out of plaster anyway.

'Bill is working in the back paddock. The boys are at school. I'm sure Mrs Harris is in the kitchen, and I believe Wayne is working at his own place today.'

Behind Jenny's courtesy was resentment. It was hard to be pleasant to Marise when she was made so aware of her undeserved antagonism. Marise prowled along the verandah, limping slightly. She had on soft soled shoes and moved very quietly.

'Actually, I came over to see Wayne.' She paused and examined Jenny. 'I've only just heard of his accident.'

Jenny schooled her face to blankness.

'It was nothing serious. He just collided with something.'

If the matter was being kept quiet, it wasn't her place to discuss it. She wondered how Marise had heard about it. Tony hadn't been around since it happened. Perhaps some of the hands had been talking.

'I suppose you had to take your turn at nursing him,' Marise probed.

'He was no trouble,' Jenny said. She felt her colour rise. 'Mrs Harris and Bill took it in turns.'

'Of course,' Marise's voice was smooth. 'I feel I should have been a better neighbour, despite the handicap of my leg. I suppose poor Wayne really roughed it with just you three to take care of him.' Jenny remained silent. Marise's red lips curled up into a sneer. 'Poor Wayne! You should have let us know! After all, Wayne is a very close friend of mine.'

'Are you staying for some lunch?' Jenny asked. 'I'm sure Mrs Harris would like to see you.'

'I'll get some lunch from Wayne,' Marise said shortly. 'Don't bother Mrs Harris.'

Jenny kept up her smile as the tall lithe woman limped back towards her car. Her face felt stiff with the effort of keeping her mouth curved the right way. Just how close a friend was Wayne to Marise, anyway?

'Has she gone?' Merry whispered behind her.

Jenny relaxed and turned around. Merry leaned against the wall like a small thundercloud, her bottom lip pushed out with disapproval. Jenny felt an odd lightening of her heart. She wasn't the only one who didn't like the elegant poised Marise Bickerton. It was odd that her duties had included looking after the children when the three of them disliked her so much!

'Yes, she's gone.' She took Merry by the hand. 'What about seeing if Mrs Harris needs some help with lunch?'

She listened with downcast eyes as Merry chattered to Mrs Harris of Marise's visit, and set the table with thoughtful deliberation. Marise's comments had rankled. Wayne didn't really seem Marise's type. Perhaps the fact that he also ran a successful property gave them a lot in common.

'Silly of Marise not to stay for lunch,' Mrs Harris grumbled. 'She won't get much to eat over at Wayne's place. At the moment there is only a station cook for the hands over there.'

'She said she wanted to see him about something,' Jenny said woodenly.

'Yes,' Mrs Harris agreed. 'Marise often asks Wayne's advice.' She gave her hearty laugh. 'Although I've never heard that she takes it. Still, Wayne seems to go along with her. It will be interesting if he actually does marry her.'

This brought Jenny back to the puzzle of Wayne's kiss. Why had he kissed her? Of course he could have been just grateful, and perhaps he was on kissing terms with every one? Did he kiss Marise, she wondered? Just the thought of it made her prickle with an undefined irritability. He might be feudal in his attitude to women, but surely he wasn't really Marise's type, with her sarcastic tongue and calculating eyes.

All through the afternoon, she kept trying to analyse Wayne's odd action. Why had he kissed her? Why was there such a watchful glint in Marise's eyes as she stressed what a close friend Wayne was? Was she trying to warn her away from Wayne? Jenny had no intention of becoming too friendly with the feudal dictatorial Wayne Paterson, even if his blow on the head had quietened him down for a few days.

She met Bill's eyes with some embarrassment when he came in for dinner, wondering if he would tease her in front of the boys. Much to her relief, he had obviously forgotten about the incident, and was full of Pretty Boy's progress.

'Tell you what,' he said expansively to the table as he waved a fork. 'If Pretty Boy comes in Allan can have his new saddle, and we're all going on a holiday.'

There was an immediate uproar from the children as they started suggesting places they wanted to see. Bill Williams laughed as he tried to quieten them, his face smoothing out into a youthful and relaxed expression. Jenny grinned with everyone else, pleased to see him laugh so spontaneously.

It was a dreadful thing to be pleased

about, but Wayne's accident had forced him out of his dazed grief, and all the hard work was helping him to adjust to the loss of his wife, and come down to the reality of getting on with his life.

'I'm dying to see him beat Black Prince,' Jenny said, still laughing. 'Are you sure it is going to be safe for me to risk my fifty cent bet on him?'

There was another outburst from the boys at her cowardice, and she and Mrs Harris defended their thrifty streaks, and lack of gambling fever. During the uproar, the odd heartache brought on by thinking of Marise and Wayne together evaporated unnoticed.

CHAPTER 7

It was Merry's birthday. Merry had graciously received her presents at the breakfast table including the matching party dress for the favourite doll. As it was a Saturday, her birthday was to be celebrated by a family picnic, at which Jenny was included as a matter of course. The clear blue sky promised a hot day, and the children had clamoured for a day at Panniken Bend.

'We'll all pile into the Landrover, and drive down,' their father suggested hopefully.

A chorus of groans greeted this suggestion. Jenny grinned at the comic face he pulled. The last few weeks had seen a startling change to Bill Williams. His eyes still had a shadow of unhappiness behind them, but he had snapped out of his earlier apathy and supervised the work around the property with brisk efficiency. This morning there was even a rueful twinkle in his eyes.

'You promised to ride,' Allan accused. 'It's no fun going on a picnic in a car.'

'And I'm going to use my new bridle,' Merry insisted, as she patted it.

'I'll go and saddle my poor retired horse,' Bill Williams said in a resigned manner.

'I already have, Dad,' John said. 'All the horses are ready, and the lunch hamper packed.'

Bill Williams shrugged, but there was a grin on his face as he let himself be jostled out of the house and down the steps by the eager boys. Jenny suspected he wasn't as averse to horse riding as he said. She watched his eyes light up at the sight of the brown gelding waiting for him.

The boys had saddled up the pretty roan mare for Jenny, and she swung into the saddle, feeling light-hearted and happy. Merry had already scrambled on to her shaggy pony. It was going to be fun to go for a picnic on horseback with the prospect of the whole day with nothing to do but laze around the river and swim. Her temporary job was proving very enjoyable. None of her other employers had included her as a member of the family in their birthday celebrations.

The birthday hamper was packed on a resigned looking pony and they set off at a sedate walk, with Merry in the lead. They had not ridden far past Taralon, when a motor bike roared after them.

The cavalcade looked around. The bike slowed and bumped alongside them before stopping. The rider raised his visor. Much to Jenny's surprise, it was Wayne. She gave him an uncertain nod. He smiled at her before concentrating his attention on the Williams' family.

'Sneaking off on a picnic without me,' he announced. 'Shame on the lot of you!'

'Did you bring me a present?' Merry demanded.

'Manners,' sighed her father.

Wayne produced a small leather riding crop, which he handed to Merry with a low bow. Merry squealed her delight, and tried to hug him. Wayne settled her back more securely on her pony.

'Coming to our picnic?' John asked.

'Of course,' Wayne laughed. 'Want a lift down?'

'I'll say!' John's face lit up. 'Come back with me while I put this four legged donkey away.'

'Can I drive down in comfort too?' enquired his father.

'It's my birthday,' Merry retorted. 'You have to ride with me on my birthday.'

'So be it,' was the resigned reply. 'Let's get moving.'

John kicked his horse into a gallop back towards the property. Wayne roared off after him.

'What an idiot,' Allan sneered. 'Fancy preferring a bike to a horse. He's mad!'

'Looks like some members of my family

are never going to shift into the twentieth century,' his father lamented, but his face was cheerful, and he patted the side of his gelding's neck as he spoke.

They were still only halfway to Panniken Bend when the motor bike returned, passing them with its extra rider on the back who waved and yelled his derision.

'I didn't know Wayne owned a bike,' Jenny remarked.

'Not many people round up cattle on horses these days,' her employer explained. 'You've been watching too many westerns, Jenny.'

'I'm going to use a horse when I take over working cattle,' Allan said scornfully. 'Bikes are stupid, and they spoof the cattle.'

'Nice to have a conservative in the family,' his father teased. 'We give away our tractor too?'

Jenny fell behind with Merry and listened in amusement as the horse mad Allan argued his case. Bill Williams had put aside his grief and looked younger today. He sat his horse with an effortless grace, and was grinning broadly at Allan's indignation.

When they reached Panniken Bend at last, Jenny's pleasure dimmed slightly. The motor bike was parked in the shade of the big gum, and a camp fire crackled away cheerfully. John was already splashing in the water.

A small boat with Marise and Tony in it was pulled to the bank. Today, they both wore tee shirts and shorts, and their resemblance was very pronounced, both tall long boned and golden skinned, with hair an almost identical shade of shining blonde.

Wayne, his brief togs revealing a bronzed expanse of muscular back, stood talking to them. Of course the Bickertons were neighbours, and country people were friendly and hospitable, and liked socialising, but for a bleak second, Jenny suddenly found her pleasant anticipation of the day clouded.

'Happy birthday, Merry,' Tony and Marise chorused.

Merry gave them a distant nod, but upon

opening the gaily wrapped box and pulling out the severe black velvet riding helmet, her face dimpled up with pleasure, and she gave an ecstatic squeal.

'Nice of you to join us,' Bill Williams said. 'Hope Mrs Harris packed enough sausages.'

'We brought a hamper with us,' Marise explained. Jenny noticed that the cast was gone from her leg, leaving a startlingly white area against the golden brown of her skin. She seemed in a pleasant mood. Her hazel eyes moved over Jenny's dusty jeans and faded shirt. 'It's too nice a day to waste working. Don't you agree, Jenny?'

'Of course,' Jenny agreed evenly, aware that her blouse and jeans were shabby, and her hair was escaping from its pony tail in untidy curls.

'Come on in, the water's beaut,' John yelled.

'As soon as we change,' Jenny promised.

She and Merry took their costumes to the thick clump of bushes to change. Merry wriggled into her brief ruffled bikini, and looked critically at Jenny's bathers.

'They're old fashioned,' she sniffed.

'Just well used,' Jenny assured her, as she folded their clothes into a neat pile.

Marise and Tony had pulled off tee-shirts and shorts, to reveal their bathers beneath. Jenny immediately understood five-year old Merry's definition of old-fashioned.

Marise wore black bathers, cut high across the thighs and plunging to a very low back. It displayed her eye-catching figure to perfection. Her skin was golden brown all over, except for the white patch on one leg and foot.

Jenny suddenly felt dowdy. Her bathers were black too, faded to almost green with age, and cut sensibly for energetic swimming. Her arms and shoulders were still lightly tanned and freckled from her previous exposure to the sun. Marise's sharp eyes missed nothing, and amusement crossed her face.

'Well,' she drawled. 'You both look very nice. Are we all going in?'

A suddenly awkward moment passed as they splashed into the water. John and Allan swung from the rope their father had tied to the tree whooping like wild Indians as they dropped into the water. Merry, after being turned back from the deeper water, got over her sulks as her father took her on his back and swam nearer the bank.

Wayne bobbed up beside Jenny and shook the water from his eyes. Today his eyes were dancing with merriment. 'Race you to the other bank,' he challenged.

Marise gave a throaty chuckle as she overheard, and she and Tony put their heads down in a flurry of foam. Tony led, and then Marise caught up, but Wayne streaked ahead to overtake them effortlessly. Jenny followed at a more sedate pace, envious of Marise's strong length. Marise swam like a fish. Wayne reached the bank and climbed out.

'Your swimming is improving,' Tony admitted as he followed him out of the water.

'Practise,' Wayne laughed, as he gave his hand first to Marise, and then Jenny to help them out of the water. 'Race you back.'

Jenny sat on the bank to regain her breath as she watched them drop back into the water and thrash back. She was content to admire their ability in the water and rest for a while.

The three heads reached shore together and argued a few minutes. Bill Williams jerked a thumb. They nodded agreement, and walked upstream.

Jenny guessed what he was advising. They were walking further upstream to have the distance to race down. She decided to walk upstream along the opposite bank to watch their race. However, soon the bush became too dense to push through. The cheerful voices on the other bank became fainter, as she moved away from the river trying to find a way through the dense bush.

A cattle track seemed to lead back to the water. She doubled over and pushed her way along the tunnel of greenery, wishing she had something on her feet. It led back to a filtered clearing by the river.

She looked through the concealing fringing of leaves down the river to Panniken Bend. It was a very peaceful scene. The river was wide on the sandy bend, and Bill Williams relaxed against a tree watching Merry splashing in the water in front of him. The boys were still swinging from their rope, and their yells came faintly as they dropped into the water. The horses dozed in the shade, and the motor bike was a bright splash of colour against another tree.

Jenny thought about the first time she had come to Panniken Bend with the children, and the creepy feeling she had of an invisible watcher. The concealed clearing was an ideal position if anyone wanted to spy on the visitors at Panniken Bend. The ground was flattened out by the bank, and she stared at the cigarette butt and half smoked cigarette in the grass. Had the mysterious watcher hidden here as he watched her?

She gave herself a shake. It was a ridiculous thought! Probably it had only been a bored angler sitting smoking as he waited for a bite. The sky was too blue, and the bush too peaceful and sunlit to even think of anything so sinister.

She followed the narrow track from the clearing. It angled away from the river and then twisted back towards the bank. The bush thinned so she could walk along the bank. She walked around the next bend. On the other side the trees were high and dense, and there was no sign of life. The river was narrower and deeper, and swirled and eddied against the high banks.

Jenny suddenly felt uneasy. She couldn't hear the whoops and yells of the boys any more, or the voices of the others who must be nearly across from her on the other bank. Ahead of her, the high stony cliffs of the ravine started. She stood on the bank and waited. This was as far upstream as the others could go. After the steep ravine was the beginning of Millalong.

Behind her a twig snapped. Jenny swung around, but there was nothing to see. She moved closer to the bank. The silence pressed down on her. Where were the others? She looked downstream and hesitated. It was a long swim back even with the current, but the thought of returning along the bank again sent a prickle of unease through her.

She looked again at the water and took a deep breath. She would swim down. Suddenly a pain exploded at the back of her head, and she fell headlong off the bank in a clumsy travesty of a dive.

The colder currents under the sunlit sparkling surface tumbled her like a rag doll. She bobbed weakly to the surface, and sobbed air into the burning ache of her lungs.

Her arms and legs thrashed aimlessly as she tried to swim towards the other bank. The current whirled her back. The water was chillingly cold, and she doubled up with cramp. She went under again. She rose to the surface for a brief second and sank again.

A strong arm caught her, and a powerful body kicked upwards beside her. Her head was lifted high out of the water.

'Stop struggling,' Wayne's voice snapped.

Her breath came in gasps. She was towed across to the bank, and lifted out. She caught a glimpse of the wary hazel eyes of Marise and the shocked ones of Tony, before she rolled over to be sick at their feet.

'What on earth were you doing swimming so far upstream?' Wayne demanded as he thumped her on the back.

'I think I fell in,' Jenny choked as she disgorged more water.

'Fell in,' Marise echoed.

'The river isn't safe this far upstream,' Tony explained. There was a worried look on his face. 'It was only luck that Wayne spotted you just then.'

Jenny sat up, and held her pounding head. Tears of shock and humiliation were filling her eyes.

'I just walked upstream to watch you swim down,' she sobbed.

'It's not really safe for swimming around this bend,' Marise drawled.

Jenny stood up and promptly crumpled again. Her knees were rubbery and her head pounded and she felt sick and giddy. Wayne sighed, and picked her up.

'I can walk,' Jenny muttered.

To her horror she realised the tears had started again. She squeezed her eyes tight shut to stop them. Keeping them shut also blocked out Marise's furious watchful face, and Tony's preoccupied frown. She hadn't been courageous enough to meet Wayne's eyes since she had been pulled out of the water.

She stopped struggling, and relaxed. Her ear was against Wayne's bare chest, and she could hear the strong thud of his heart beating. His body was warm and his arms held her securely, so securely she had dropped into a state of relaxed drowsiness by the time they had reached Panniken

Bend. Wayne was very efficient, and settled her by the fire with a rug around her, and soon she was drinking a hot mug of sweetened tea.

'I think we should take you home,' Bill Williams suggested.

'Don't be silly,' Jenny scoffed. 'It's Merry's birthday. I'll be all right in a little while.'

Gradually her shivering stopped. Lunch was cooked, and Marise and Tony produced an elegant cold chicken and shared a bottle of white wine with Wayne and Bill. She steadfastly refused anything to eat. However later in the afternoon, after Merry's cake was produced, and the candles lit and blown out to the lusty accompaniment of everyone singing happy birthday, she felt almost normal, and was relieved she hadn't ruined everyone's enjoyment by going home.

Wayne roared off on his bike to return driving the Landrover. His suggestion that the children come with him and Jenny and leave their father to bring back the horses, was howled down as a tame way to end a picnic. John offered to ride Jenny's horse, so Jenny ended up the only passenger in the Landrover.

'See you at the race meeting,' Marise promised, as she and Tony pushed their boat back into the water.

Everyone waved a cheerful farewell. Marise and Tony rowed the boat rapidly upstream where it slid around the first bend and vanished from sight. Wayne then drove Jenny back to Taralon in a silence neither of them seemed inclined to break.

Mrs Harris had hot scones and a cup of tea ready, and was shocked to hear of Jenny's accident.

'You do look whitefaced,' she exclaimed. 'Why don't you go straight to bed.'

'I'm all right,' Jenny protested. 'I just got a fright.'

They sat in the kitchen and drank tea, and waited for the others to arrive back. The sun began to set and there was a faint chill in the air. The light gradually faded. The strained look was back on Wayne's face, and several times he sneaked a look at his watch.

Jenny kept her eyes on the riders coming over the hill. The horses were moving fast to reach the comfort of their stables. She wondered if Wayne kept watch on his property too after dark, but his face was aloof and reserved, and she didn't dare ask. The riders cantered closer, and Merry swerved her pony across to the verandah.

'I raced everybody home,' she squealed. 'Are you having a birthday dinner with us, Uncle Wayne?'

'Not tonight,' Wayne said. He stared down at Jenny, an intent considering stare, and his eyebrows came together in a scowl. Jenny, flushing at the way she had curled so comfortably in his arms when he had carried her, avoided his gaze. 'Take it easy for a few days, Jenny Wren.'

He stood up and put on his helmet, and a few seconds later was a fast vanishing figure on the bike roaring off into the darkness.

Jenny and Merry headed towards the bathroom. Merry was silent and sleepy as

Jenny bathed and changed her. Jenny was silent too. She had a lump swelling at the back of her head as proof she hadn't lost her footing and fallen into the river.

She had a lot to think about. She had been hit on the head and pushed into the water. If it hadn't been for Wayne, the mysterious attack could have caused her death. The question was why?

CHAPTER 8

Jenny stretched cramped legs as the station wagon braked. The weight of the horse float on the back meant they had travelled slowly, and the drive into Warrnambool seemed interminable.

It was the weekend of the big race meeting, but only Jenny, Wayne, Bill Williams and the strapper were in the station wagon. Wayne was driving. It was the first time Jenny had seen him since the day of the picnic, but he had only given her a casual nod as she got into the back seat, and confined his conversation to Bill Williams and the strapper.

The children watched them leave in a state of mutiny. Allan had brought mumps home from school, and given them to John and Merry. Except for John, who was really ill, the others were over the worst, but Mrs Harris flatly refused to allow them to go to Warrnambool for the weekend.

'No point infecting everyone in the district with mumps,' she scolded as she herded them back to their rooms. 'And leave Jenny alone. She is entitled to a break after nursing you mob all the week.'

Jenny was a bit dismayed that Mrs Harris and the children weren't accompanying her for the weekend, but her decision to stay at the property with Mrs Harris and the children was greeted by disbelief.

'Most of Taralon is booked into the usual pub,' Bill Williams said blankly. 'It's the one event of the year the whole district attends! Of course you're expected to come. You don't want to miss watching Pretty Boy win.'

'Well if you put it like that,' Jenny conceded.

She was in a cheerful frame of mind as she packed her yellow chiffon dress for the dinner dance, two cotton dresses and hat for the race meeting, and her new blue jersey halter-neck for the ball. It seemed so long since she had gone anywhere, or had any excuse to dress up that she was looking forward to the social weekend.

Her temporary job had now dragged out to eight weeks, and apart from the occasional horse ride she had not been off the property at all. The last week of nursing the children had been very tiring. They had been fretful and demanding, and there was still no sign of Marise returning, although she seemed completely recovered from the accident.

When the ramp of the horse float was lowered, Pretty Boy was nervous and distrustful. It took the three men careful handling to back him out of the float. The grinning little jockey, who was to ride him the following afternoon, arrived to inspect him.

'Looking good,' he remarked.

Pretty Boy swung his head around at the voice, and his ears went back. The little man spoke again in a soft voice, and Pretty Boy, recognising the voice, moved forward to allow himself to be coaxed into his stable by the jockey.

'Is Ben sleeping with Pretty Boy?' Jenny asked, as the strapper grabbed a bedding roll out of the back of the station wagon.

'He and every other strapper in Warrnambool,' Wayne explained. 'They all worry someone might have designs on their precious horses.'

'Stealing!' Jenny asked.

With the strapper gone, Bill motioned her to move into the front seat with them. He slid behind the wheel. Wayne moved beside Jenny, and she was aware of his casual arm behind her resting on the back of the seat. Without the horse float, the station wagon moved with unaccustomed smoothness.

Wayne smiled at the shocked expression on Jenny's face. She felt herself smile back. She guessed Wayne was looking forward to the weekend's relaxation too. He seemed more cheerful, and his face looked carefree and untroubled.

'Now who could dispose of a glut of stolen racehorses? They all worry someone might dope the horses before the big race.'

'Is there really any danger of that?' the startled Jenny asked.

'Mainly imagination,' Bill Williams said drily.

He turned the station wagon into the crowded car park beside the old fashioned hotel with its wide verandah and wrought iron edging. Bill Williams was actually whistling to himself. Wayne winked at Jenny as he got out and collected all the cases. Jenny grinned. It was nice to hear Bill Williams sound so happy. Today the habitual strain on his face had faded. She guessed he was also looking forward to the weekend.

Later Jenny unpacked in the room the motherly proprietor had escorted her to. Mrs Macka was actually a sister of Mrs Harris and knew about the mumps. Like everyone else she took Jenny's presence at the meeting for granted.

'I changed the rooms around as Adelaide and the children aren't coming up, but you'll be quiet enough here,' she said with her comfortable smile. 'We've put all the hands in the other wing where they won't disturb us.'

The weekend was going to be fun, Jenny decided. They had arrived in time for the race meeting this afternoon. Tonight there was the dinner dance, and tomorrow after the main race meeting everyone was going to the ball. She went over to the window and looked out. Her room faced on to a cobbled courtyard, with the garages around it. Further over she could see the roof of the stable complex with the fenced yards surrounding it.

Cars moved in a steady stream along the road that led to the racetrack. Jenny glanced at her watch. She had promised to be changed within the half hour. It took her a little longer, but she surveyed her reflection in the mirror with satisfaction.

The dress she wore was one of her favourites. The blue deepened the colour of her eyes, and the fitted bodice and full skirt showed off her small waist. She brushed her hair and tied it back with a blue ribbon. Remembering about the amount of walking everyone did at the races, she slipped on her flat heeled white sandals.

The rap on her door sounded imperative. She grabbed her wide brimmed white hat and rushed out. It was Wayne who had knocked. The well cut light weight suit he had changed into made him look a stranger. She had become used to seeing him dressed more casually. For some inexplicable reason there was a rueful look in his eyes as he inspected her.

'Didn't mean to keep you waiting,' she apologised.

'No problems,' he drawled. He tucked her hand into his arm. 'Let's go. Bill's got the car out the front.'

She sat between the two men in the front seat and they set off. As they drove along, the men kept waving and calling greetings.

'There can't be any of your neighbours left home,' Jenny remarked. 'Look, there's the Sellmans! They must have their entire six kids crowded in the van.'

'Every single hotel, and boarding house is packed full for the racing carnival. Of course everyone is here,' Bill Williams laughed.

'Have Marise and Tony brought Black Prince up yet?' Jenny asked.

'They would have come up at the beginning of the week to settle Black Prince in,' Bill said. 'They like to be here for the full racing week.'

'I'm sure you'll see them both at the race course,' Wayne said drily. 'They never miss any of the races.'

He had spoken so drily that Jenny flushed, and felt the familiar antagonism rise again. There was a silent rebuke in his remark, but she again decided that Tony's friendship was certainly no business of his.

Once they arrived at the crowded race-track, their progress was slow. Jenny had met some of the neighbours during her stay, but a lot more had stopped to greet them and had to be introduced.

Wayne sounded resigned as he introduced Jenny to the light-hearted group who gathered around her. More and more neighbours and friends gathered, and Jenny was slowly edged away from Wayne and Bill Williams.

A firm hand clamped around her waist. There was a chorus of indignant protests. Jenny turned. It was Tony, blond hair ruffled in the wind, and his hazel eyes snapping in temper. His words were light enough.

'I have come to rescue you from these uncouth types. I might have known they would home in on you.'

Jenny tried not to show her annoyance at his possessive attitude. 'Exactly like a knight in armour,' she said sweetly.

The tall red headed boy with freckles, who had been introduced as their neighbour on the property to the west of the gorge was indignant.

'Fair go Bickerton,' he stammered. 'Like you to try to monopolise our new arrival. We're going to show her some proper country hospitality.'

Tony waved them away with an aloof expression. 'She doesn't need your chicken sandwiches and flat champagne, she's dining with me.'

'I'm supposed to be lunching with Bill Williams and Wayne,' Jenny apologised to the circle of disappointed faces.

'And they are waiting,' Tony reminded her as he swept her away from the group with more haste than courtesy.

Jenny promised to meet them all again at the dinner dance, and looked at Tony in exasperation. He was pulling her through the crowded course. Bill and Wayne had vanished completely from her sight. Tony caught her glance and slowed down. The brooding expression vanished and he grinned. Without the tense irritability on his reckless changeable face, he looked young and very carefree. She grinned back.

'That's better, Jenny Wren,' Tony said. 'You don't want to waste time with that mob – very boring.'

Jenny laughed outright. There was no point in taking Tony seriously. Sometimes he seemed as young as Allan, sulks and tantrums included. She was still laughing as they entered the dining room.

Bill Williams waved from across the room, and motioned to the two empty chairs at the table. Wayne and Marise were sitting together, and didn't look up until Tony pulled the chair out for Jenny to sit down.

Wayne nodded an unsmiling acknowledgement. Jenny felt her smile fade as she nodded back. Marise gave Jenny and her brother a measuring stare, and turned back to continue her low voiced conversation with Wayne.

Jenny sat down. So Wayne didn't like Tony! It really was time he improved his manners, and kept his dislike under control in a more civilised manner. Jenny turned her back on him and concentrated her attention on

Tony, who murmured outrageous compliments into her ear.

Marise, immaculate in a well cut green linen suit suddenly became gracious and talkative. There were no barbed comments to Jenny, or derogatory remarks at her brother. The conversation started to flow more easily. An outsider would have said it was a very pleasant luncheon party. Jenny was still wary. Marise in a good mood seemed insultingly patronising, and as difficult to take as Marise in a bad mood. After lunch, Marise was the first to rise.

'I want to get some bets on,' she explained.

Wayne murmured something to Bill, and followed her out, and they were quickly swallowed up by the crowd. Tony and Bill Williams resumed their discussion of training methods.

Jenny sneaked a look after Wayne's retreating back. He hadn't even bothered to glance in her direction as he left. Her cotton dress, which she had put on with such pleasure, now looked childish and un-sophisticated beside the sleekly tailored green linen suit of Marise. Jenny pushed back her hair. The heat had caused it to straggle from its ribbon and curl around her neck. Marise's hair was twisted up in a sleek roll with not a silken golden hair out of place!

'Marise is getting him well trained,' Tony jeered. 'Wayne hates chasing around the betting ring, and he went off without a murmur.'

An unpredictable mood swing had darkened his face as he stared after them. Bill Williams glanced across at him, his light coloured eyes suddenly intent. Tony became aware of his gaze, and gave a forced laugh.

'Just joking,' he muttered. 'Are we going to watch the next race?'

Bill Williams shook his head, and gestured for a refill of his coffee. He obviously was going to stay where he was for a while.

'You were going to show me the saddling enclosure, before I risk my hard earned wages on a bet,' Jenny reminded Tony.

'A good suggestion,' he agreed, his face lightening.

He pulled back her chair. Bill Williams nodded an absent goodbye to them. He had settled himself comfortably to study the racing guide. Tony slipped a possessive arm around Jenny and guided her out of the dining room and into the hot sunshine.

Jenny put her unaccountable depression firmly behind her. Wayne Paterson seemed to be as moody and changeable as Tony, but nothing was going to spoil her weekend out! She gave Tony a bright smile.

'What about we back something with long odds?' she suggested.

CHAPTER 9

Jenny wriggled her feet out of her high heeled slippers and hid her stockinged feet under the table. The dinner dance had been fun, but it was getting late, and she decided she was tired.

The two blond Sullivan boys, and the freckled redhead called Terry had claimed acquaintance with flattering enthusiasm. She spent a lot of the evening going from table to table and being introduced, and dancing with everyone.

Tony and Marise were on a table with a crowd of older people, most of whom spent the evening drinking heavily. Tony had danced with her earlier in the evening, and then been ousted by the Sullivan boys. Marise shrugged a disdainful shoulder as she danced past, and Tony stayed the rest of the evening among his particular friends.

At last Jenny refused all offers to dance, and returned to sit down. Most of the revellers were packing up, and the dance floor had a curiously forlorn look to it with the trampled streamers and shredded pieces of coloured balloons. She was alone. Bill Williams stood on the floor trying to disentangle himself from an elderly gentleman who had buttonholed him. Wayne leaned over a table on the other side of the room talking to friends.

He seemed to be very well liked, and had spent a lot of the evening socialising with everyone. When the dancing started, he danced twice with the nice Sullivan girl, and several times with Marise. Jenny wondered if he was going to offer to dance with her, but first Tony had whisked her onto the floor, and then the other boys had crowded Tony out and monopolised her.

Tony was dancing with his sister. Jenny watched with an unwilling admiration. They had the floor almost to themselves, and danced with the perfect coordination of professional dancers or born athletes. Marise's white chiffon swirled around her lithe body as she moved. Tonight her shining hair was twisted back into a soft Grecian knot, which revealed the perfect regularity of her features, and softened her face. She looked very regal and self assured, and definitely the most striking woman in the room.

The music stopped, and there was a spontaneous round of applause. Marise gave her flashing smile. Tony moved over to ask Bill Williams something. He nodded agreement. Marise returned to her friends, and Tony headed across to Jenny.

'I offered to take you back to the hotel, Jenny,' he explained. 'That prosy old bore will have Bill trapped until the first race tomorrow.'

'What about Marise?' Jenny asked.

She tried not to look across to where Wayne was laughing broadly at something the older of the Sullivan girls was saying to him on the other side of the room.

'Our table is staying at the same hotel, and she isn't ready to leave,' Tony said with a shrug.

Jenny slid her feet back into her slippers and picked up her black velvet wrap. She smiled at all her new friends as Tony took her arm and walked her outside to where the rakish red sports car was parked.

Jenny tensed as Tony flung the car out of the car park at what seemed a dangerous speed. She opened her mouth to protest, but then shut it again. In the glow of the dashboard Tony's eyes had a bright glitter to them. If he wasn't drunk, he definitely had been drinking, and to comment on it was unnecessary for the short distance from the hall to the hotel. She remained silent, wrapped in her own thoughts.

It had become fairly obvious that the Bickertons weren't too well liked. Behind the good natured tolerance and courtesy of the greetings was a uniform coolness. Jenny had overheard a few outspoken and scathing comments about both Tony and Marise. The least damaging remark was that Marise was an unpleasant tongued snob, and she and Tony were extravagant and reckless in their lifestyles and property management.

Yet Wayne, who was so level headed and popular, not only escorted Marise around the racetrack, but caused comment by his attention to her at the dinner dance. Was there really something between them? An odd pain contracted her heart, as she remembered how well they danced together, and the intimate lazy way Marise smiled up at him.

The car skidded to a halt in the car park in front of the hotel, and she shivered. Perhaps it was because she was tired, but suddenly she felt depressed.

'Cold, Jenny?' Tony sounded concerned, and pulled her velvet cloak closer around her.

Without thinking, Jenny moved away. Tony shrugged, got out and walked around to open her door. Jenny was embarrassed. Tony's silences gave away a lot more than his speech did. They walked together along the dimly lit verandah.

'Got your money on Pretty Boy, to-morrow?' he asked.

'The last five dollars I own,' Jenny retorted, relieved at the safeness of the question. 'I'm not a betting lady, but I think he will win.'

Tony put out a hand to stop her. He was swaying slightly.

'Lay you odds that Black Prince will win.'

'What odds?'

His arms went around her. 'The odds that we become a lot closer friends.' Jenny started to back away. He tightened his grip. 'What about it, Jenny Wren?'

'You're being ridiculous. We already are friends.'

'Yes I know,' he agreed, breathing the acrid combination of whisky and beer in her face. 'I mean proper friends.' Jenny stiffened as he pulled her close and kissed her, and her wrap slid from her shoulders. 'Why waste your time making sheep's eyes at

Wayne. Marise has him.'

'It's late, Tony.'

Jenny tried to keep her voice level and dispassionate, but she felt close to tears. Although it had been difficult she had tried to treat Wayne the same way as everyone else, and his involvement with Marise didn't affect her. Why should Tony, who had too much to drink, come out with such a ridiculous statement?

'Not that late,' Tony chuckled thickly.

He settled his shoulders comfortably against the wall, still holding her in his iron hard grip. He bent his head to kiss her again, and his hand slid over to fondle her breast. Jenny raised a foot to stamp down hard. Suddenly Tony released her, and spoke over her shoulder.

'Nice night.'

Jenny whirled around. Wayne and Bill Williams had come up quietly behind them. Her cheeks went hot, and she wondered what they had overheard, or what they were thinking.

'Goodnight,' she gasped, and escaped Tony's arms to the sanctuary of her room.

She threw herself on the bed. An odd misery constricted her heart. For some inexplicable reason she felt guilty and shamed. Yet it was no one else's business, so why the silent disapproval in the two men as they followed her into the hotel. She was a free agent. Her employer couldn't dictate who her friends should be! And what business was it of Wayne's who kissed her?

Jenny sighed, and wiped away a stray tear with a firm hand. She slowly undressed and hung up her dress. In her frantic flight to her room she had forgotten to pick up her black velvet wrap. She knew exactly where it had fallen. It must be on the floor of the wide verandah just by the front door.

She opened her door. The intense stillness of the hotel greeted her. The idea of tiptoeing down the quiet passageways and silent stairs in the darkness just for her wrap seemed ridiculous. Although she wouldn't like to lose it. Even the soft hood was fully lined in the white taffeta, and she had never seen that design again since she bought it. She decided to slip down first thing in the morning and collect it. She shut the door again and went to bed to pass a night of uneasy broken slumber.

She slept late, and woke the next morning with a vague sense of depression. She stared at the unfamiliar high ceiling of the room, and memory flooded back of the incident of the previous night. Also, today was the big race, and she had promised to be ready early.

She showered and dressed and rushed down to the dining room. It was deserted, and she stared in horror at the ornate clock on the mantel. She had overslept! It was already eleven o'clock. She ran down the winding passage to the lounge.

Bill Williams was sprawled in a massive arm chair studying the paper. He glanced up as she came in. There was only an amused friendliness in his face, and Jenny felt herself relax.

'I didn't realise I had overslept,' she apologised. 'Are you taking Pretty Boy to the racetrack?'

'Hours ago,' he laughed. 'Ben and Wayne are babysitting him. I came back to collect you.'

Although her employer protested, Jenny refused to delay him by eating and assured him she could eat at the track. She was already sitting in the station wagon, before she remembered about her evening wrap.

'I dropped my black velvet wrap on the verandah last night,' she explained. 'Did you notice if it was still there this morning?'

'It was left folded over the stair rail,' Bill Williams said. He slid her a shrewd glance, in which compassion and worry were equally blended. 'It's in the office.'

Jenny wrinkled her brow. Who had picked it up and left it on the stair rail? A later come guest that night, or perhaps someone who came down in the morning ahead of the cleaning staff? It was odd that they hadn't put it by the small office! She dismissed it from her mind as they parked in the crowded car park of the racetrack.

'Are we going to have a look at Pretty Boy first?' she demanded.

'He seemed a bit miserable this morning, so I do intend to have another look at him,' was the explanation.

When they arrived at the complex of saddling yards, Ben the strapper grinned a shy welcome. Wayne looked up and nodded without speaking. Pretty Boy flicked an ear in the direction of the new arrivals, but otherwise ignored them. His coat was as glossy as usual but his eyes looked dull, and his head drooped with disinterest.

'Could be the strange surroundings,' Ben suggested.

Bill Williams nodded. He checked each leg carefully, and ran his hand carefully down the powerful shoulders. He looked puzzled, and his light blue eyes were worried.

'Seems all right,' he admitted. 'What sort of a night did he have?'

Ben shrugged. 'You saw him when you

both came back last night. He had settled in real well.' He appealed to Jenny. 'Didn't he look all right to you?'

'I didn't come down here last night, Ben,' Jenny protested. 'I went straight in to bed.'

'You wanted to pat him for luck,' Ben insisted.

'What time?' Wayne demanded.

Ben scratched his head. 'Suppose about half an hour after you and the boss came through.'

Jenny stared at Ben. It wasn't like him to make anything up. How could he say he saw her last night?

'Did you slip down later to have a look at the horse?' Wayne asked.

'Ben was mistaken,' Jenny insisted. She could feel the tell tale flush colouring her cheeks again. Why did Wayne always have to make her feel in the wrong? 'I certainly didn't come down to the stables last night!'

'It was you,' Ben insisted. 'All muffled up against the cold in that fancy black cloak and hood.'

Jenny just stared at the young strapper. There was a silence. Ben looked embarrassed, Bill worried, and Wayne's brows had come down in their straight bar. The distant blare of the band started, and Pretty Boy's head lifted and his ears pricked forward.

'I daresay it isn't important,' Bill Williams said with a shrug. 'He looks a bit brighter doesn't he? I swear he recognises that band.'

Ben grinned his agreement, and stroked the raised head. 'Won't be long, old fellow. Today is your day.'

'He's got a few hours to settle down,' Wayne said.

'I'll stay with him,' Bill Williams announced. 'Take Jenny up for something to eat. The dining room should still be quiet.'

Wayne took Jenny's arm. 'An odd coincidence,' he said smoothly, as soon as they were around the corner and out of earshot.

'What's that supposed to mean?' Jenny snapped.

'Two Jennys around last night!'

Jenny was grateful for her large floppy hat, as the colour rose in her face at his accusation. 'Ben's getting things confused. I wasn't there last night.'

'Ben's pretty reliable. I don't think he got anything confused,' Wayne drawled.

'I didn't go down to look at the horse last night,' Jenny repeated, hearing her voice rise and sharpen.

'If Pretty Boy comes in, the winnings will help balance the books over the stock losses.'

'I know that.' Jenny was bewildered at the change of direction of the conversation.

'Just who are your loyalties with, Jenny Wren?' Wayne asked coldly.

'What's that supposed to mean?' Jenny retorted.

'I mean your very close friendship with Black Prince's owner?'

Jenny stopped walking and glared at her escort. She could feel her temper rise at the unfairness and pettiness of the remark. Not even from Wayne Paterson had she expected to hear such a ridiculous insinuation.

'You practically live in Marise's pocket. Is your friendship a disloyalty to Taralon too?'

'That's different,' Wayne snapped.

'I bet,' Jenny scoffed.

She turned and marched away from him through the crowded race course. Wayne lengthened his stride to keep up. She was too angry to even speak. She blinked back the treacherous tears prickling behind her eyelids. What business was it of Wayne's who she was friendly with? She sneaked a look at him.

His mouth was compressed into a grim line, and the telltale bar of brows down over his cold grey eyes. So he was worried about what was happening around the district, and anxious that Pretty Boy wasn't in top condition, but why was he overreacting so childishly? He became aware of her quick glance.

'You disgust and disappoint me,' he exploded at her. Jenny pulled her hat further over her face and ignored him. His hand suddenly tightened around her arm, so she was forced to stop. 'Afternoon Marise. Like some lunch?' he asked in a completely different voice.

Jenny examined Marise. She stood by the dining room entrance, elegant and self possessed. Today she wore a tailored white linen dress, and a shady hat to match. What was supposed to be special about Wayne's friendship with Marise? Why was he so paranoid about her brother?

Marise gave her flashing smile to Wayne, and slid a hand over his arm. 'What a good idea,' she said.

'Lunch it is,' Wayne said heartily, still holding Jenny's arm in the vice like grip. 'I'm sure Jenny is hungry.'

The dining room was beginning to fill, but they found a table near the door. Jenny studied the menu. A lump in her throat took away any appetite she had had, and she was resentful under Marise's amused eyes, inspecting her soft lemon voile dress, and the flat heeled white sandals. Marise had the ability to make Jenny feel like an untidy fourteen year old! Marise concentrated her attention back on Wayne.

'Black Prince has had the week to settle in like a lamb.' She studied the menu thoughtfully. 'How is Pretty Boy this morning?'

'Looked all right when we left him,' Wayne remarked, and changed the subject to the other owners and their horses and prospects.

Several times during the meal, Marise came back to the subject of Pretty Boy, and the sort of money they were putting on him. Each time Wayne steered the conversation away. Jenny ate in silence. Wayne made no attempt to include her in the conversation, and Marise ignored her as though she was invisible.

As soon as possible after eating, Jenny got up quietly and left the table. There had been undercurrents in the conversation that made her uncomfortable. Marise's questions were probing, and Wayne casually and lightly deflected them, still with the amused smile on his face.

Also, although Jenny was not prepared to admit it, Wayne's transition from the pleasant courteous and likable man she had nursed into the tense and sarcastic stranger struggling to keep an undercurrent of violence under control puzzled her. The incident of being kissed by Tony was really a very trivial thing for him to be so inexplicably upset about.

She noticed as she left the dining room that her departure was unnoticed. They were totally immersed in their odd guarded and bantering conversation. Jenny straightened her shoulders and went out into the bright glare of the hot sun, among the cheerful jostling crowd.

It really was too nice a day to let either Marise or Wayne get under her skin.

CHAPTER 10

People pushed and jostled, totally preoccupied with their racebooks and pencils. Jenny glimpsed Terry and two of the Sullivan girls over by the rails. She considered joining them, and then hesitated. They were fun to be with and very friendly, but somehow she wasn't in the mood for their carefree exuberance.

She let herself be buffeted and pushed towards the brightly coloured umbrellas of the bookmakers. Everything was fast moving, exciting and noisy. The bookmakers bawled their odds, and eager men and women surged around, grasping crumpled bundles of money. In the tight packed seething mob, so much money flashed so carelessly lost its reality, almost like Monopoly money, Jenny thought, her eyes wide at the abandon with which it got pushed at the bookmakers and their busy clerks.

She listened for a while. The odds on Black Prince and Pretty Boy were shortening. In the betting ring they had settled to being equal favourites. Everyone in the district seemed to be putting their money on one or the other of the two horses. Jenny recognised many of the station hands and neighbours milling around.

She was glad she had decided to place her five dollars for Pretty Boy more sedately at the T.A.B counter. She lost interest in the betting, and was pushing her way out of the crowded betting rings when Tony erupted into sight, glasses slung over his shoulder, and inevitable racebook in his hand. His face lit up as he spotted her.

'That hat, Jenny!' he exclaimed. 'No wonder I couldn't find you.' He shot out a firm hand to hold her. 'Now, don't run away on me.'

Jenny gave him a level stare. He looked

excited and carefree. There was not a trace of embarrassment about him over his behaviour of the previous evening, or hadn't he remembered?

'She forgives me, she forgives me not,' he chanted, peering under her hat brim to look into her accusing blue eyes.

'She forgives you not,' Jenny said stiffly. Then she thought of how silly she sounded, and gave an unwilling smile.

'That's better,' Tony approved. 'Have you been fed?'

Jenny assured him she had, wondering how she could make her escape without being too obvious. In her present mood, Tony's company lacked appeal. The problem solved itself as he glanced at his watch.

'Have to get back to report to Madam. I've backed Black Prince with our last remaining shirts.' He hesitated and pulled her around to face him, his eyes searching her face with a curious intentness. 'Interested in the odds I quoted last night, Jenny?'

'Definitely not.'

The indignant refusal caused him to narrow his eyes, and his grasp on her arm became iron hard. He opened his mouth to say something, but the loudspeaker drowned him out. He tensed and released her. 'This is it, Jenny. See you later.'

He turned on his heel, and disappeared through the crowds. The loudspeaker chanted out scratchings, weights and riders. Jenny listened with half an ear as she pushed towards the rails. She had decided that just in front of the winning post was the best position to watch the race from. A woman in front of her in a flowered hat, checked her book against the loudspeaker's gabbled information.

'Pretty Boy scratched,' she remarked to her companion, an elderly lady in similar floral hat.

Jenny came to a shocked stop. Had she really overheard correctly? 'Excuse me, please!' she stammered. 'Did you say Pretty Boy?'

'Scratched,' the woman agreed without looking up from her book. 'He was favourite too.'

Jenny turned and forced her way through the crowd surging towards the fence. Bill, Wayne and the strapper had all seemed confident that Pretty Boy was improving when she had left them. What was happening?

The loudspeaker rattled out more of the race information. She realised absently that Black Prince had drawn an inside position. His chances of winning had suddenly improved dramatically. He had a good barrier position, and the only horse capable of competing with him was out of the race.

Jenny quickened her pace towards the saddling paddock. She caught sight of Bill Williams. His face was grim and tense. He was hurrying towards the office. Jenny ran to catch up with him.

'Bill,' she called.

'Now now, Jenny,' he said curtly. 'Be a good girl and wait in the stand.'

Jenny sighed, but hurried back to the stand, climbed the steps, and sat down. She eavesdropped on the two men in front of her discussing the scratching.

'Pity,' one said. 'Pretty Boy was the favourite.'

The other man checked his racebook, and wrote something down. He shrugged. 'My money is on Black Prince. The odds were getting too short anyway.'

'Someone said the swab was positive.' There was a knowing note in the shorter man's voice.

'It will come out at the enquiry,' was the indifferent reply.

'Lining up for the big race of the day,' the nasal voice boomed over the loudspeaker.

A sudden hush fell over the course. There were the magic words, 'They're off!' Jenny stood and strained her eyes to distinguish the horses as they raced past in a tight bunch. The crowd was noisy again, and the loudspeaker shrieked the race performance over its roar.

The coloured silks of the jockeys were an indistinguishable blur. The horses were moving further apart as they galloped around the track. A bunch of four leaders appeared, and the other horses dropped further and further behind as they came around the second time.

Jenny clenched her fists and stared until her eyes watered. She wished she had binoculars. Two horses levelled out neck to neck for the home run. Was it the flamboyant orange and black of the Bickerton colours fighting to the front? The horses flashed past the winning post, and still she didn't know which one won.

'Looks like being a photo,' the man in front announced.

'Silver Sound ahead by a nose,' the other man said. The loudspeaker crackled out the winner and place getters in agreement. 'That's an outsider, if ever there was one. Told you Black Prince was too erratic a performer, despite his speed.'

The two men moved away. The race was

over and the stand emptying. Jenny sat down again, and prepared for a long wait. At least Black Prince came second! Would Marise and Tony be disappointed? Had they backed him straight out or for a win? They were so confident of his ability to win. A hand tapped her shoulder. It was Bill Williams. He looked tired and more stooped than ever.

'What happened?' she asked as she followed him down the steps and out of the stand.

'The swab was positive,' he said flatly. He sighed at her blank expression. 'Pretty Boy was doped.'

'That's impossible!' Jenny gasped. 'He was never alone.'

'Impossible or not,' he said as he ushered her across the car park and into the station wagon. 'The swab was positive. Certainly enough of the drug was still in his blood-stream to slow him down.'

Jenny was silent. She had read about cases of rigged races and doped horses, but never had any first hand knowledge of it before. She remembered all the money that changed hands at the betting rings. People stood to make or lose big money on horses. With so much money at stake, racing became big business, even when the owners only entered the one horse as a hobby.

'Who would do such a dreadful thing?' she asked at last.

Bill Williams remained silent. Her heart sank at his grim expression. His silence was more damning than any accusation. Who stood to gain by Pretty Boy's doping? The only horse capable of challenging Pretty Boy was Black Prince, or the outsider Silver Sound. Would someone have invested so much money that it was worth their while to get Pretty Boy out of the running? She shivered, and suddenly the sunlit carefree crowds jostling around acquired a darker side. Had a sinister and ruthless underworld syndicate decided to remove a threat to their investment?

Of course Tony admitted he and Marise

had backed Black Prince for a lot of money. That suspicion was dismissed immediately. Owners always backed their own horses to win. The Bickertons were reputable property owners and neighbours of long standing. Among the close knit community such a deed was unthinkable.

She stared again at the crowds of light-hearted racegoers and holiday makers. The idea of staying for the ball seemed repugnant. She wasn't in the mood to enjoy dancing all night, and the light-hearted celebrations.

'Would it be possible for me to get a lift back to Taralon this afternoon?' she asked suddenly. 'I don't particularly want to stay for the ball.'

'I'll see if the Sellmans will drop you back,' her employer returned. Was there a slight easing of the grim lines of his face? 'They will be going back some time this afternoon, and Taralon isn't that far out of their way. Wayne and I are staying for the enquiry. Will you be all right?'

Jenny nodded. Bill dropped her at the hotel and drove away. She went up to her room in a subdued frame of mind. She changed back into her shirt and jeans and packed her clothes slowly. She came down to the loungeroom with her case to wait. Mrs Macka took back her key and assured her there was nothing to settle, as her stay was covered by the Taralon family company.

'Don't forget your wrap, Jenny. Isn't it a shame about Pretty Boy. No wonder no one feels like celebrating. Who are you going back with?'

Jenny explained that she hoped to get a lift with the Sellmans, as Bill Williams and Wayne were staying in Warrnambool for a few days.

Mrs Macka nodded a comfortable agreement. 'It shouldn't be out of their way. Would you like a cup of tea while you wait? It's going to be a long drive back in their old van.'

Jenny smiled agreement. She folded her wrap and dropped it on top of her case. It was hardly worth unstrapping her case to pack it. Mrs Macka arrived with the tea tray, and Jenny sat alone in the silent lounge. It was not long before the Sellman van tooted its summons, and Jenny and her case were settled in the very back between the two older boys.

It was a long slow trip back. The Sellman boys were too shy to say anything, and old George Sellman concentrated on his driving. She was glad when they reached Taralon at last. Mrs Harris offered the Sellmans tea as they pulled up to unload the weary Jenny and her case, but old George Sellman refused with a smile, insisting he wanted to get his family home before dark.

'I haven't had a chance for a gossip with Connie for months,' the disappointed Mrs Harris said watching the van bump away. 'What happened to Pretty Boy that they scratched him? Some of the hands are saying he was doped?'

Jenny shrugged, and said she didn't know any more than what was going around the race course. It was Bill Williams's place to fill everybody in on what happened. She certainly wasn't courageous enough to even hint that perhaps he suspected that the Bickertons or anyone else he knew might be behind the doping of Pretty Boy.

As she unpacked her case, Jenny paused as another thought struck her. Why had her employer made the special trip to drop her back at the hotel? She knew he was worried, but why was he so grim and silent as he returned her? Surely the trip to return her to the hotel immediately wasn't necessary? She could have waited until after the race meeting finished.

She sensed his relief when she volunteered she wanted to go straight back to Taralon. Why? Had he really believed Ben's statement that she had visited the horse the night before the race? Did he suspect her too? What if someone wearing her wrap had tricked Ben to relax his vigilance so they could dope Pretty Boy?

The thoughts went around and around in

her mind. She started to feel sicker and sicker. Who found her evening wrap and left it folded on the stair rail? Because she had accompanied Wayne and Bill for one last check of the horse on the way to the dinner dance, Ben had seen and admired her black evening wrap. He sounded so sure that it was her he had seen that night!

The food stuck in her throat. At last she excused herself to Mrs Harris and went straight to bed. Perhaps after a good night's sleep all the dark forebodings clouding her mind would shrink to manageable proportions.

She was just drowsing when she heard the distinctive purr of the Mercedes at the front. What was Wayne doing back here? She lifted her head from the pillow and listened. She heard Wayne's curt quiet voiced orders, and the lower rumble of agreement as he and two other men walked down past the side of the house. With a shock she realised she had pushed the ever recurring worry of the cattle rustlers to the back of her mind. The hands on the property were still keeping watch! Only a few minutes later she again heard the distinctive purr of the Mercedes as it started again, to fade quietly into the distance.

Jenny relaxed, but sleep was longer in coming. She kept puzzling over what dreadful urgency had caused Wayne to get a lift back back to his property to collect his car, drive to Taralon, and then leave immediately for the three hour drive back to Warrnambool. Just what was going on?

CHAPTER 11

'Please, Merry, take yourself and your dolls off the desk,' Jenny suggested, trying to keep her voice even and good humoured.

Merry pouted, and sat a large and extremely ugly doll on her knee, ignoring the request. It was the week following the race carnival. The boys had recovered from their mumps and were back at school. Merry, bereft of their company, was bored and demanding.

'Why don't you take a carrot down to Bertha,' Jenny suggested.

The little shaggy pony, Merry's pride and joy was originally named Birthday Boy, which shortened to Bertha.

'He's not supposed to have carrots.'

Jenny gave up, and closed the heavy ledger. She had set herself the task of doing the books to take her mind off the ever present worry of how the enquiry was going. The days had passed and the rumours and conjectures flew around the place, but no one knew anything. Now there was an expectant uneasy silence over all the hands at Taralon as they went about their duties.

Bill Williams had phoned with the message he was staying in Warrnambool until the enquiry was finished, but the enquiry had finished, and still no one knew what was happening. One of the station hands volunteered the information that Wayne was back working his own property. If he came back at night to check the security arrangements of Taralon, Jenny hadn't seen or heard him.

Only Mrs Harris seemed immune from the tension that had everyone so grim-faced.

'No point going off half baked,' she said stolidly. 'We'll hear the facts when Bill comes home.'

The weekend had come and gone, and still

Bill Williams hadn't returned, and Merry had suddenly become possessive and demanding. She was bewildered by the continued absence of her Uncle Wayne, and the suppressed impatience and tension in the atmosphere wasn't helping. Jenny studied her bored and sulky face.

'What about we go blackberrying?' Jenny suggested.

Merry's face brightened, and she scrambled off the desk, dolls tumbling in all directions.

'I'll get my special bucket. I know where there're lots and lots of blackberries.'

'Watch out for snakes,' Mrs Harris warned as she came out to see them off.

'And we can have blackberry tart for tea,' Merry decided.

She scampered down the steps ahead of Jenny, clutching her bucket, her earlier boredom completely gone. School would be good for her, Jenny mused to herself. She was much too intelligent to be left to her own devices all day.

This thought had her wondering about the intentions of Marise. She appeared to have completely recovered from her accident, and yet there was no sign of her returning to work at Taralon. No one had seen anything of her or her brother since the race meeting. They had stayed in Warrnambool for the week of the racing carnival, despite the rumours that they had lost heavily when Black Prince was beaten.

'Always Sydney or the bush with those two,' Mrs Harris had sniffed. 'Their money would have been all up on Black Prince winning. Still, owing everyone won't stop them enjoying themselves.' With which comment, she had returned to whisking her egg whites with a suppressed energy.

Not many people at Taralon seemed to actually like the Bickertons, and the children actively disliked Marise. Yet Gwenda Williams must have liked her. They had got very close in the six months before the accident, Mrs Harris had said. Jenny tried to visualise the dark haired bride of the wedding photograph as Marise's close friend. Gwenda Williams would have been at least twelve years older than Marise, and the wedding photograph, despite the likeness to Wayne revealed a face with vulnerable gentle eyes, and with a childish almost petulant droop to the full mouth.

Could Gwenda Williams have developed into the sort of sophisticated malicious personality to be compatible with the younger Marise? Somehow Gwenda seemed too like her brother to be Marise's type. Her mind strayed to the shape of Wayne's firm mouth. It was definitely the same mouth, but firmed into a controlled strength, and the same shaped lower full lip hinted at sensuality rather than petulance. Would that mouth soften into warmth and tenderness when he kissed a woman properly?

'It is hot,' Merry grumbled. 'After we pick our blackberries, can we cool down by the creek? I bet there's no silly old snakes down there.'

Jenny blushed, suddenly aware of where

her thoughts were taking her. For just a few seconds, her treacherous imagination had her actually being kissed by that warm controlled mouth with its disturbing hint of sensuality.

'You're looking awfully hot too,' Merry insisted. 'Is it all right if we go down the creek to cool down afterwards?'

'If there are no snakes there first,' Jenny agreed.

She followed Merry down the hill to the creek paddock, where the blackberries clustered in a last defiant uncleared tangle. Soon her temporary job at Taralon would be finished. In fact, after Christmas, Merry would go to school with her brothers, and there would be no real need for Marise to bother to return. Now that Bill Williams had recovered, he could easily cope with the bookwork.

She would go back to the Agency for another position in the business world of enclosed spaces. Somehow strolling after Merry across the dry hot paddocks of

Taralon under the hot blue of the sky, her previous existence of office temping seemed unreal and dreamlike.

The reality was filling brimming buckets with the juicy blackberries and stopping Merry from eating too many as they picked. After they had filled both buckets, they found a shady spot by the creek to have a rest. Jenny checked for snakes, before she and Merry sat with their bare feet in the water which trickled over the clean washed stones. Apart from the murmur of the water the silence was absolute, and Jenny felt herself relaxing. She had been unaware that the tension over Taralon had affected her so physically.

By the time they trudged back with their full buckets, appetising smells drifted out from the kitchen. The battered station wagon, with the horse float still attached, was parked by the stables.

'Dad's home,' Merry yelled, flinging herself up the stairs, and spilling black-berries from her over full bucket.

Jenny followed more slowly, picking up the blackberries. Bill Williams sprawled comfortably on the old couch in the kitchen drinking tea. Mrs Harris was at the table rolling pastry, a wide smile showing the gold fillings in her teeth.

'What happened?' Jenny asked, interrupting Merry's breathless recital of the lizard they saw.

'The enquiry found Pretty Boy doped by a person or persons unknown, administered about twelve hours before the race.'

'All that time away just for that!' Jenny exclaimed in puzzlement. 'You knew that before the enquiry.'

'Merry looks as if she has more blackberries on her than in her bucket,' Bill Williams said, changing the subject.

'Time both of you cleaned up,' Mrs Harris prompted, shifting cakes out of Merry's reach.

'Uncle Wayne's come,' Merry announced looking out the window.

Jenny followed her glance. Her heart sank

as she saw the grey Mercedes slowing by the front steps. What did Wayne think of the findings of the enquiry? Why was Bill Williams so tense and uncomfortable? Was there something he was keeping back? She took Merry's hand, grateful for the excuse to go.

'Come on Merry. We'll get cleaned up.'

'Haven't seen Uncle Wayne for ages,' Merry chattered, as she splashed in her bath.

'Everyone's been very busy.' Jenny kept her voice casual. 'What about coming out?'

Soon Merry danced off, very pleased with herself in her pink velvet dress, with a huge bow in her hair. Jenny got herself bathed and changed.

She put on a fresh cotton dress and stared blindly at the mirror as she brushed her hair. Why had Bill Williams sounded so evasive and uncomfortable? Did he or Wayne believe she was involved in the doping of the horse? She remembered the curious comment he had made about the two Jennies around the night of the dinner dance. Just the merest glimpse of Wayne was making her feel prickly and uncomfortable, almost guilty, she thought to herself. Going in to dinner felt like an ordeal.

After their roast lamb and vegetables, came blackberry tart and cream for dessert. With the boys and Merry, the conversation around the dinner table was boisterous and general. Apart from one level glance, Wayne concentrated his attention on the boys and Merry.

Afterwards Jenny took the coffee tray out to the verandah, and the two men drifted after her to relax in the sagging cane chairs. Merry and her brothers stayed in the loungeroom by the television. Jenny jumped straight into the thoughtful silence.

'Anything come out about the woman Ben thought he saw leaving the stables?' she demanded as she poured out the coffees.

The two men exchanged glances, and Bill Williams filled his pipe, his eyes on his fingers as he tamped the bowl.

'Ben didn't mention it,' he explained.

'He said he saw someone,' Jenny insisted.

'In a black velvet wrap and hood,' Wayne drawled.

'You see, Jenny,' her employer explained. 'Although anyone could have borrowed that wrap that night, it sounded sort of nasty to mention it.'

Jenny stirred her coffee and realised what he had said. It was to protect her that the incident of the visitor in the black velvet wrap had been suppressed. Someone was able to plunge a syringe into Pretty Boy, and walk off unchallenged. It was pretty obvious that Ben believed it was her! And what about Wayne. She sneaked a side look at him.

'You think I did it?'

Bill Williams put his cup down precisely on the saucer, and fumbled to light his pipe. It had gone out again. He glanced at Wayne, but Wayne remained silent.

'Ben said he saw the back view of someone in your hooded wrap, reach up to the

179

horse's neck, and then walk away without answering him.'

Jenny became aware of Wayne's damming silence. There was a tenseness to his posture. Did he really believe she was guilty?

'Don't worry about it,' Bill Williams advised as he stood up. 'There's always another race meeting for Pretty Boy. Time to check the patrols.'

The two men went down the steps to vanish into the dusk. Jenny sat for a while, and her coffee grew cold. She gazed across to where the dim glow of lights outlined the stable area.

So Ben did believe it was her that night! Even if he hadn't mentioned it at the enquiry, he probably discussed it among the hands now they were back. Perhaps everybody on the property were weighing the pros and cons of whether it was her or not? The very fact that her employer asked Ben to suppress any mention of the incident made it look as if she was guilty and Bill

Williams was protecting her.

Wayne's belief in her guilt was obvious. His dislike of her friendship with Tony was suddenly clear. The Bickertons were the only ones with a motive for disabling Pretty Boy. He must believe that Tony was behind the doping, and she had helped him. The hot blood rushed to her face and then she shivered in the evening breeze. Surely not even Wayne could believe that of her? She collected the tray and took it into the kitchen.

The next few days were miserable and depressing. Jenny was hard put to pretend an air of indifference to the coldness that had spread through everyone on the property towards her. The stock was still disappearing despite all the precautions and night watches, and somehow it made it all worse, as though she was to blame.

Mrs Harris was cool and impersonal, and the station hands wary and embarrassed. Conversation always stopped when she came near. The children seemed bewildered.

'What's up with Ben and the boys?' John demanded outright in his blunt manner.

He had spent the morning at the stables helping with the horses, and returned with a ferocious scowl on his normally good natured face. Allan shuffled uneasily at his heels and watched Jenny out of the corner of his eye. He nudged his older brother and whispered something. John went scarlet, and with a muttered apology turned on his heels and fled to the security of the kitchen.

Jenny was hurt beyond words at the boys' actions. Surely they didn't believe the gossip too? She walked back to the house with a heavy heart.

She felt so terribly isolated. Wayne hadn't been around for days. Sure proof that he believed in her guilt, she thought dully. Bill Williams was too preoccupied with his missing stock to do more than greet her as he passed. She hadn't seen Tony or even Marise since the race meeting. For some reason they were keeping clear of Taralon. Not that she cared, she told herself. Unless it was proof that they had heard the rumours too and believed them. And what of the Sullivans, and that nice Terry? Did they believe the rumours flying around?

She thought longingly of returning to her home and the smooth anonymity of temporary office positions. Her mother's last letter had pointed out she had been away for nine weeks, and surely she would be home before Christmas! Then again if she went back, it would look as if she was leaving because she was guilty. She just had to stay and wait out all the unpleasantness. She clenched her fists as she thought about it.

How had her life managed to become so complicated and unpleasant?

CHAPTER 12

There were a succession of clear hot days, each one hotter and brighter than the day before. Jenny paused at the door of the office and looked out. The sky was an unclouded brazen blue, and waves of heat shimmered around the gums and over the brown of the paddocks.

'It's hot,' Merry complained, tagging at her heels with an armful of dolls.

'Yes,' Jenny agreed.

It was still early morning, and she was determined to get the books finished before the heat of the day turned the little office into an airless oven.

'Mrs Harris is looking for you, Merry,' Wayne said as he came up silently behind them. 'She needs some help with her cake making.'

Merry put her dolls on the battered couch and ran towards the kitchen, an excited gleam in her eyes. It was very seldom there was an invitation issued for her to help in the kitchen.

'Into the office, Jenny Wren. I want to talk to you.'

Jenny was surprised, but obediently stepped over to the chair at the roll top desk. Wayne shifted the dolls and sprawled his long length on the couch.

He didn't begin at once. He picked up one of Merry's dolls. It was bald, and still had strips of sticking plaster rakishly across its head. He inspected it carefully. Jenny waited in silence. Wayne had moved back into his usual room at the house these last few weeks. He was always courteous and somehow impersonal if he spoke to her, but for some reason his aloofness hurt. This morning he looked grim, his brows black bars across icy grey eyes. Jenny's heart missed a beat at the expression on his face as she waited for him to speak.

She knew why he was looking so grim. All the men at Taralon looked grim, tired and worried these days. She knew from her bookwork that the continuous and inexplicable disappearance of stock was proving a drastic financial problem. The outwardly prosperous Taralon was bleeding internally from the remorseless loss of the marketable cattle. Now the promise of a long hot early summer was threatening more problems and expense as the necessity for hand feeding the remaining stock loomed closer.

'Jenny,' he began. 'We've appreciated how helpful you've been over the last two months, but the arrangement was only temporary.'

'Marise is actually coming back?' Jenny asked in surprise, realising that this was a prelude to her dismissal.

'I don't think we'll need Marise's help from now on. Merry will be at school after the holidays, and Mrs Harris will be able to manage.' A flush spread over his face, and for a few seconds the icy grey eyes were averted. 'We're very grateful for all your help over a very difficult period, but I think it's time you left.'

Jenny was puzzled by his discomfiture. Of course she wanted to go home, but if Marise wasn't coming back, she should stay at least until the boys broke up for their holidays. Then she realised why she was being asked to leave! An odd pain twisted in her heart.

'You're sending me away?'

He looked even more uncomfortable. He put the doll back carefully on the couch beside him, still not meeting her eyes.

'I think it would be better if you left now.' He waited, but Jenny just stared at him. He sighed, inspecting the polish of his boots, and said bluntly. 'If you're gone, all those nasty rumours floating around should die a natural death.'

'What about Merry, and the bookwork?' Jenny managed stiffly. So he did believe she was guilty of doping Pretty Boy!

'Everything is pretty much under control now,' he assured her. 'Bill can get back to handling the paperwork, and Merry is old enough to be sensible. Bill and the children would be delighted if you kept in touch with Taralon and be very pleased to see you again whenever you want to visit, but after all this unpleasantness is over.'

Jenny stared at him. She felt cold all over despite the warmth of the room. The hurt spread and spread. The still air carried the reassuring sounds of Taralon going about its normal business; a motor coughed its protest in the distance; the cockatoos squabbled noisily in the big gum, and Merry's high pitched treble and the lower murmur of Mrs Harris's voice came faintly from the open window of the kitchen.

For a few seconds her sense of reality faded, as though she was isolated and deafened by the senseless repetition of her pain. He did believe she was guilty! She clenched her fists and took in deep breaths of the warm dusty air. Then the tight knot in her stomach eased. She wasn't guilty and Wayne Paterson had no right to expect her to wear the mantle of that guilt. The anger and defiance flooding through her straightened her back and flushed away the pain.

'If Marise isn't coming back, you still need someone until the holidays,' she said crisply.

Wayne raised his eyes from their inspection of his boots. The black brows flew upwards. The grey eyes got a gleam in them.

'Your services have been dispensed with,' he reminded her.

'Bill can make it his first job in the office to make up my final pay when school finishes,' she announced. 'Mrs Harris is going to be too busy to look after Merry until then. Unless,' she challenged. 'You're accusing me of incompetence?'

'I've never said that,' Wayne drawled. 'Bill and I just wanted to protect you from any discomfort.'

'I think I'm the one to decide whether I'm uncomfortable or not,' Jenny snapped.

Wayne stood up suddenly, his face black with rage, and leaned over her, his face so close that Jenny could see the twin figures of herself reflected in his enlarged pupils.

'I don't think you have as much sense as Merry,' he gritted. 'Otherwise you wouldn't have put yourself or us in this situation.'

'Rubbish,' Jenny exclaimed shortly.

It was obviously the wrong response. Wayne took a deep breath, and two iron hard hands fastened on her shoulders, and lifted her to her feet.

'So generous with your favours, Jenny Wren,' he drawled. 'Why waste them on someone who was only using you?'

Jenny didn't waste her time trying to pull free. She glared up into his face. 'I seem to remember telling you once that what I do is no business of yours,' she retorted. 'I happen to be old enough and perfectly capable of looking after myself.'

'Good,' Wayne said with a short laugh. 'Thanks for the invitation.'

Without warning his mouth was suddenly on hers, and she struggled ineffectually to pull away. His kiss was brutal and hard, forcing her mouth into compliance. One of his hands touched the side of her neck, paused, and continued down to unbutton the front of her shirt. She shivered, waiting for his hand to move down to claim her waiting breast, deafened beyond rational thought by the thunder of her pulse.

Her knees felt boneless, and she relaxed against him, tilting her head back. The mouth on hers softened, and the kiss became slower and more tender. She was shaking, but she was not sure why, and she felt the tremors through his body as she pressed against him.

Suddenly he pushed her away from him, and firmly down in the chair. His brows met in the familiar black bar, and his grey eyes stared into hers like a bewildered stranger. Jenny tried to draw in deep sobering breaths, and buttoned her shirt with a shaking hand. For a few seconds she had felt as if she had been on an irrational high. Why hadn't she kicked him hard in the shins when he started to manhandle her, or at least slapped his face as hard as she could?

'You owe me an apology,' she stammered.

For a few seconds she thought he was going to shake her, he looked so startled and furious. His hands tightened around her shoulders. Just then her employer came into the office.

'Ill treating the hired help, Wayne?' he said mildly.

Wayne flushed, let go of Jenny, and turned on his heel.

'She won't go,' he flung back as he strode away.

Her employer sat down on the vacated couch and took out his pipe. He tamped tobacco in and made several attempts to light it before it caught. Although he looked tired and strained, he looked better than when she had first met him. Now his face was alert, and there was a humorous twinkle in his pale blue eyes.

'I'll leave when the holidays start,' she insisted. She wanted to add she didn't care about the gossip or the malicious rumours, and this was the only way she could show her innocence, but as his worried doubtful expression crept back, she didn't dare. 'It's all right,' she reassured him.

The expression on his face relaxed. He stood up and put a kindly hand on her shoulder.

'I'm going to have to do that wretched bookwork when you're not here. Take a break and go for a ride.'

Jenny felt herself relax. At least Bill Williams believed she was innocent. He had only been worrying about trying to protect her. She felt the relief and happiness spread through her, and she gave him a radiant smile.

'A young woman with guts,' he said as he smiled back. He took her place at the desk and pulled the heavy ledger towards him. 'Take Buttercup,' he suggested. 'She's overdue for some exercise.'

Jenny grabbed a riding helmet, and went across the yard to the stables. She saddled up Buttercup with a feeling of anticipation.

It seemed to have been weeks since she rode. She swung into the saddle and held the eager Buttercup back to a smart trot as she left.

The property looked sleepy, basking in the early morning sunshine. There was no sign of activity. Most of the hands were down in the back paddock checking stock. A few horses grazing by the creek twitched their ears as she rode past, but there was no other sign of movement.

She swung the gate shut after her, and cantered along with a feeling of release. Everything was very quiet, even the birds were silent, and the fine powdery dust rose behind her. Gradually the tension, and the miserable inexplicable ache in her throat vanished. She felt a sense of gratitude for her employer's suggestion that she go horseriding. It was just what she needed to blow away the past weeks of gloom, doubt and depression that had hovered over her so blackly.

She reached the winding track beside the

river. It was cooler here, and the trees gave welcome shade. Buttercup plodded on, her earlier friskiness under control. Jenny let the reins go slack, and Buttercup moved in her own direction and at her own speed.

This, she realised was a farewell ride. She would look forward to seeing her family and home again, although her few months of working here made her realise she was a country person. She was going to find it hard to settle back into city life again. She mused on the possibility of getting more work on a country property, and then shook her head. She couldn't see herself as a Jillaroo, and she knew that a position like this was not likely to turn up again at the agency.

She tried to keep her mind away from the memory of Wayne's inexplicable actions, but deep inside her something savoured the way he had trembled as he held her. What right did he have to be jealous? Was it jealousy or just his chauvinistic arrogance which had set off his lovemaking. It was lovemaking, she admitted to herself. She remembered the way her treacherous body had stopped fighting his kisses and shivered. It certainly was time she went home to her well ordered and satisfactory life of temporary office jobs. Except, office work no longer seemed satisfactory. She mused about moving her life in a different direction. She was young enough to take on another profession. Wool classing, or horticulture might lead back to country living.

Buttercup ambled onwards. Jenny was not watching the scenery. One gentle bend gave way to another, and one group of gum trees reflecting the water, gave way to another. There was a soothing sameness to the river as Buttercup followed the trail around. They reached Panniken Bend, and Buttercup veered inland past the dense bush.

The riverbank started to chop up into deep gullies and stony winding creeks, with clumps of rocks rearing in massive forma-tions. The ground was rising to the high stony plateau which divided the start of the

Millalong property from Taralon.

Jenny came back to the present with a start. She understood why the Bickertons had boated down to the picnic ground. It would be hard to pick a track around the boulders, crevices and ravines across to the river.

She checked the horse. It was really time to start moving back. The sun was directly overhead and glaringly hot on the unshaded rocky ground. She looked at the way the ground sloped down in front of her between sheer walls.

Buttercup had drifted well inland. She looked back over the hot mass of tumbled rocky ground. She could cut back and across the top of the plateau until she came out on the road that led to the back paddock at Taralon, but it would be a long hot unshaded ride. She turned in the saddle. She could go back, but how far into the tumbled mass of broken ground had Buttercup ambled? She had been in such a deep reverie she hadn't noticed how far she had come.

She studied the slope in front of her again. It looked as if it led around the tumbled mass of rock, and back to the river bank. Mind made up, she urged Buttercup down the slope. It was going to be a lot more pleasant to find her way back along the shade of the riverbank, than cut cross country.

Buttercup moved forward placidly. Around them the ravine sides rose higher, and the ground became stony. The natural corridor wound and twisted with other fissures crossing it. After a while Jenny got worried. She was now sure it was leading away from the river.

She reined Buttercup. The last thing she wanted to do was get lost in these desolate gorges. They covered a lot of the countryside, and even locals sometimes took the wrong turning.

She was turning Buttercup around when she heard the sound of cattle. She paused and listened. Sound was deceptive among the narrow winding walls, but somewhere not too far away were cattle.

'And cattle means someone's property, and a property means a road,' she told Buttercup, as she urged the horse forward.

Around another corner, she stopped. A stout railing fence barred her way. She tied Buttercup to the rail and climbed over. Around the next bend, the high walls widened out to enclose an unexpected paddock. She kept on walking to skirt cautiously around the cattle milling around. Cattle usually dozed in the midday sun, but these were restless.

A small jet black poddy calf bellowed. With a sudden shock, Jenny recognised it. It was one of Merry's favourites, and she was inconsolable when it vanished with its mother and other cattle one night a few weeks earlier.

Jenny inspected the cattle more carefully. It could have been Taralon stock, but she wasn't sure. She knew the black poddy calf and she thought she recognised a gaunt cow with a broken horn. Had she stumbled on the stolen cattle, or were they strays? She remembered the stout railing fence and bit her lip. The fence meant that the cattle in this paddock, were confined, not strays!

The high stony cliffs reared in an unbroken wall, and the paddock curved around below it. Jenny kept on walking, curious to see where it led. The paddock opened out again into another longer area, narrowing down at the other end with a high barred gate. Beyond it the fissure wound out of sight behind the concealing walls.

Against one side of the paddock was a solidly built small wooden hut. Beside the one straggling tree, was a large closed cattle truck with its ramp down. Two men watched two riders on trail bikes herding cattle up the ramp. The tailgate was then lifted into position, and the men wrestled briefly with the catch before climbing into the cabin.

One of the figures got off the trail bike and walked to the front of the truck to give something to the driver. The other trail bike roared over to the high barred gate and opened it. The truck rumbled through and vanished from sight. The gate was swung shut after it.

One trail bike was pushed into the open shed, and the other rider rode back and into the shed. The two riders came out. One of them pulled off the obscuring helmet to throw it into the shed, and ran a hand through shining blonde hair. It was a very familiar gesture. The other figure threw his helmet into the shed as well, and shut and bolted the door.

Jenny gasped. The other figure had short hair which gleamed in the sun. Despite the hot sun a chill went through her. She realised who was behind all the cattle smuggling! The well hidden paddock in the lonely desolate gorges and the black poddy calf were damning evidence.

She stepped back against the shadow of the cliff. The movement caused both heads to swing around. There was something ominous in the way both figures sprinted towards her with such desperate speed.

Jenny wasted a valuable second wondering what Marise and Tony would think about a witness to their smuggling activities. She then turned and fled along the winding paddock towards where she had left Buttercup tethered.

CHAPTER 13

'Jenny,' Tony called sharply.

Jenny ignored him, and kept on sprinting around the herd of cattle, causing them to shift uneasily. She risked a quick backward glance as she ran. Tony and Marise were catching up fast. Even in that panicky moment, the reluctant admiration welled up. Marise ran as freely and smoothly as an athlete, the shining hair flowing behind her.

Jenny flung herself on to the fence, one hand releasing Buttercup's bridle. Another few seconds and she would be away. Not even Marise could keep up with a galloping horse. Without showing her pace Marise scooped up a stone and threw it. It landed on Buttercup's rump with a thud. The bridle slid through Jenny's fingers as the startled horse galloped off.

Marise reached Jenny ahead of Tony, and grabbed her wrist. Jenny struggled to pull away, off balance with one leg over the fence. Her heart sank as she heard the sound of Buttercup's hooves fading in the distance. Marise pulled her off the fence and flung her towards Tony who caught her arm in an iron hard bruising grip.

'Take your little spying playmate,' she said coldly.

Jenny's breath came in sobbing gasps, but Marise wasn't even winded. Tony's eyes met his sister's, and a hidden message passed. Jenny looked from one to the other and the chill at the pit of her stomach spread and spread. The Bickerton twins were extra-ordinarily good looking, with their magnificently coordinated bodies, shining blonde hair and regular featured faces, but it wasn't the contemptuous dislike in Marise's face causing her to feel so sick, it was the dawning horror on Tony's face. Why was he so horrified, and refusing to look directly at her?

'Tony,' Jenny pleaded.

'Shouldn't spy, Jenny,' Marise sneered. She slid off the fence, and captured Jenny's other hand and jerked her into movement as they walked back, around the milling cattle and the curve of cliff towards the small hut.

'I recognise some of the stock in that herd,' Jenny accused coldly.

Anger started to swamp her apprehension and stiffened her back. The fear and panic faded as she stared at Marise. Everything added up. The district gossip about the Bickertons' extravagant tastes, and the vague assumptions that they were subsidised by overseas wealth. The continual leakage of stock from all the neighbouring properties as well as Taralon.

The desolate gorges isolating one side of the Bickerton property made a perfect place to hide all the missing stock. No wonder that road blocks and truck checks revealed nothing. The stolen cattle would be whisked a few kilometres to the hidden paddock, held until everything settled down, and then disposed of.

'Thieves,' Jenny sneered. 'How very inelegant!'

Her outburst was ignored. She was dragged closer to the hut. Tony hesitated then, his face dark and moody, one hand tight around Jenny's wrist.

'Can't afford to be squeamish,' Marise reminded him as if in answer to the unspoken plea in his eyes. 'Even if she was cooperative, and she's not!'

Tony shrugged, his face setting into grim lines. He stared down into Jenny's face for a long second. His eyes were sombre, ruthless and impersonal. Jenny stared back. Without the mask of careless good humour Tony looked an unpleasant stranger, bitter and desperate and a lot older. The sort of person who would also dope racehorses.

'How did you manage to get to Pretty Boy?' Jenny demanded.

'All done with your help Jenny,' Tony said, even white teeth showing in a mirthless smile. 'Ben was quite prepared to trust your evening cloak, if not Marise under it.'

Jenny thought briefly of all the misery and unpleasantness she had endured those last weeks; the malicious rumours, the slights, and the covert appraising stares of neighbours who wondered if she was guilty.

'What a pity there still isn't a death penalty for smuggling,' she said distinctly. 'You deserve prison for life.'

'No extradition treaty,' Tony explained.

'Hurry up,' Marise ordered, as she dragged Jenny up to the doorway of the hut. 'We've got to get that last lot out this afternoon. Time could be running out.'

They flung Jenny through the doorway. She fell sprawling on the dirt floor and the heavy door slammed behind her. She heard the bolt slide across. She picked herself up and hammered against the door. It was solid wood planking. She yelled and yelled, and her voice echoed around the enclosed wooden space. No one answered.

She sat down again with her back to the

wall and tried to control her panic, and steady the racing thud of her heart. What did they intend to do with her? The words 'no extradition treaty' and 'time's running out' hammered at her brain. Of course they intended to leave the country, and soon, but what was going to happen to her? Marise's words, 'can't afford to be squeamish' suddenly acquired a more sinister meaning.

She shivered, in spite of the airless heat of the hut. Surely they wouldn't murder her in cold blood? The cold voice at the back of her mind reminded her that this couple who had grown up in the district had been systematically thieving and cheating their neighbours. She represented a danger to them, and the efficient Marise would certainly find a way to silence her.

Jenny prowled around the hut. The solid roof had heavy rafters with tin nailed over them. There was no window. The thin line of daylight through the gaps in the planks showed only the two bikes and the hump of an old saddle in one corner. There was nothing else.

Even if the Bickertons didn't kill her and left her locked up here while they escaped the country, she could starve to death before she was found. This paddock was tucked away somewhere among the impenetrable ravines and gorges of the plateau. No one knew of its whereabouts.

Jenny pushed the hair out of her eyes, and tried to control her frantic thoughts. The more she thought about her situation the more her head ached. There seemed absolutely nothing she could do.

The slow hot hours dragged on. Soon it would be dusk, and then no one had any chance of finding her! Even if and when Buttercup arrived back at Taralon, no one knew in which direction to start searching. Bill Williams probably believed she was somewhere near the river.

During the long afternoon, she could see with one eye pressed to a narrow chink between the planks as the trucks came and went. Each of them stayed long enough for their load of cattle to be herded on board, and then rumbled off again.

Jenny's eyes flicked around the darkening hut, as she tried to think of a way out. She had tried to scrape a hole under the wall with her bare fingers, but the ground was iron hard. It was going to be dark so very soon, the light was fading. She huddled down and put her head into her knees.

She just had to think, and stop these waves of panic from flooding over her. If only she could light some sort of fire? Any smoke in the district always brought someone up to investigate. An untended fire was dangerous at this time of the year, with the grass and bush so tinder dry.

She sighed. She never carried matches with her. She went through her pockets carefully. All she had was a handkerchief. She strained her eyes through the darkness of the hut. The trail bikes had petrol in them, but it wasn't much use without matches. Her eyes focused on the shapeless mound of the old saddle. Saddles had saddle flaps sewn into them, and most of the old stockmen smoked!

She squatted beside the saddle and checked the pockets under the saddle flaps. She found an old check handkerchief, dirty and stained, some grey waxed thread, and a flattened half empty packet of matches. She pulled the saddle away from its corner. Beneath it was an empty chaff bag.

Her fingers shook as she frayed string off the sacking and twisted it together. She unscrewed the petrol cap off the tank of one of the bikes, and dipped one end of the string down. All the time her mind worried at the problem. If she could push the thread through under the gap of the door and light it, would it catch on the long dried grass outside?

The rumble of another truck became louder. If this last batch of cattle were spirited off, there would be nothing except her word against the Bickertons to connect them with the rustling. On her second try, the match flared, the frayed string caught, and a cheerful flicker glowed redly in the darkness. Her hands trembled as she fed it under the door and waited. Nothing happened!

She put her eye to the chink in the door and tried to look down. Surely there would have been some smoke if it had caught? She tried to steady her mind to think more clearly. Would the petrol cause it to flare too quickly, without catching the grass? Outside the truck was stopped, and the sound of the herded cattle thudding up into the truck was very close to the hut. A mounting urgency made her fingers clumsy as she frayed some more string off the chaff bag.

This time she made sure she had a healthy blaze going without using the petrol, before pushing the clumsy string under the door. It must catch! It was her last and only hope. The flame flickered higher and she fed it the strayed string, the ruddy flames lighting every corner of the little hut. Then she pushed the rest of the long string through the chink in the planks, too absorbed in her task to feel the flames as they scorched her fingers.

The pungent smell of burning grass mixed with the musty smell of dried wood reached her. The dusk had a reddish glow, and there was the sudden crackle of dried grass, and the snap of twigs burning.

Jenny found another chink in the wall to peer through, and gave a sigh of relief. Within her limited range of vision she saw the flames creeping towards a desiccated clump of bushes. Clouds of smoke billowed up into the still air. Smoke that would alert everyone that a fire had started.

The billowing heavy smoke drifted back under the narrow gap of the door, and through the splits in the planking, to catch her throat and make her eyes water. Surely there shouldn't be so much smoke in the hut? There was no wind!

She tried to place her eye against a gap in the wall to see, but leaping flames obscured her vision. She drew in her breath sharply.

The hut was on fire! She screamed and beat on the door. The heavy smoke kept billowing under the door, and the loud crackle of the flames devouring the dry planks of the door sounded vicious.

Could anyone hear her? Why didn't they come? Of course it would suit the Bickertons to have her burn to death in an unexplained fire, but surely the men helping load the stolen cattle wouldn't ignore her screams? Jenny gasped for breath, and strained for a breath of clear air through a narrow crack on the opposite wall.

In the limited vision of the gap, she distinguished Marise's lithe body, swaying backwards and forwards as she fought the flames. The fire was halfway down the paddock, and three other figures were outlined against the red glow fighting the fire.

Jenny screamed again, and hammered on the door. It was hot to touch, and the tears poured down her cheeks as she coughed. An engine started up with a full throated roar.

Jenny put her eye back to the narrow crack. She saw Tony's tense face illuminated by the flames as he pointed at something. Marise nodded agreement. More and more shadowy figures appeared silhouetted against the flames. Jenny hammered on the door and screamed again. Surely someone would rescue her? There seemed a lot more people fighting the fire. Where had they come from?

The bolt slid back, and the blazing door was flung open. She stumbled out into Wayne's arms. The flames lit the horror on his face.

'How did you end up here?' he snapped.

'The Bickertons locked me in. How do you think?' she snapped back, and promptly burst into tears.

'Hush, Jenny,' he soothed. 'It's over now. Don't cry.'

Jenny clung to him. She had never felt anything as safe and secure in her life as his hard body against hers. She clung as if she would never let him go. She tried to control the shudders sweeping over her.

'The truck,' she wept. 'It's gone.'

'Not too far,' he drawled. His face was lit with a wide grin that made him look surprisingly young. 'Bill and the others were waiting.'

'You knew all the time,' Jenny accused. She tried to draw back to look at him, but his arms were remorselessly tight holding her against him.

'We weren't sure,' he said as he smoothed back her hair and produced a handkerchief. 'We had to wait to catch them with the cattle.'

Jenny looked over his shoulder. The paddock swarmed with people. The grass fire was out leaving a blackened smouldering expanse, but behind her the hut was a lurid bonfire that lit the surrounding paddock.

A group of men checked the cattle, which milled around at one end of the paddock. Marise and Tony stood together, watched by another group of men. A truck was parked in the shadows by the high barred gate.

Bill Williams came over. There was a smile on his face that made him look almost carefree. Jenny tried again to pull away from Wayne, but his arms were too tightly around her.

'All of the last lot of two year olds back,' he gloated. 'Not only have we got them all, but the racket in the stolen stock is broken.' He looked severely at Jenny. 'You are the limit, Jenny Wren. I thought I was keeping you out of the way.'

'You knew about the Bickertons all the time?' she said indignantly.

'Only suspicion,' he was quick to disclaim. 'It was Wayne who remembered about the secret paddock. It seems the Bickertons blasted a gap through to drive the trucks in. It made a perfect hiding place.'

He glanced around. The paddock was emptying. Men were herding the cattle towards the narrow end of the paddock.

'It's a fair walk, Jenny,' he apologised. 'We couldn't bring any vehicles too close. Are you all right to walk out?'

'Of course,' Jenny said, taking in deep breaths of the heady air of relief and freedom.

'You can head home with Ben and some of the station hands,' Bill Williams continued. 'We have to take this lot to the local lock up.'

'I'll see her home,' Wayne drawled.

Bill Williams looked at the way Wayne had Jenny so securely tucked under his arm. Jenny flushed at his grin, and the way he winked at Wayne before turning on his heel. Wayne grinned back, and with Jenny still closely against him, they walked towards the high barred gate.

The parked truck was empty of cattle, and the Bickertons and three other men were huddled into the back, together with grim faced neighbours as guards. The tail gate was put up, and the truck rumbled off into the darkness.

Wayne and Jenny joined the slow procession of neighbours and cattle through the widened fissure of the gorse. Jenny recognised the cheerful faces of the Sullivan boys and Terry.

Ted recognised them and gave a grin. He also looked amused at the tight grasp Wayne had around Jenny.

'Police are in for a busy night.'

'Do them good to do a bit of work for a change,' Wayne said cheerfully.

The fissure wound and twisted through the darkness. After a while it narrowed and turned. Jenny peered at the raw freshly blasted walls. At last they pushed through a dense screen of willows. They were at the creek, and on the side where the dense screen of willows followed the creek around, just under the apparently unbroken wall of plateau a portable bridge led across the creek.

'Oh,' Jenny gasped in comprehension.

'Exactly,' agreed Wayne. 'Straight up the creek, and into the gorge. Vanished without a trace.'

They kept walking across the paddock. When they reached the main road Jenny saw a convoy of cars, trucks and bikes parked there. More cattle were being disgorged from the hemmed in trucks, and neighbours milled around sorting out stock.

'The car's over here,' Wayne explained.

He opened the door and she sat down in the grey Mercedes with a sigh of relief. She felt as if the day had gone on forever, so much had happened.

'Did Buttercup get back?' she asked.

'No problems,' Wayne assured her.

He drove back in silence. Soon they reached the house, where the lights glowed their welcome through the darkness. Wayne slowed the car to stop by the verandah steps.

'Thank you for driving me back,' Jenny said primly.

Wayne turned off the car lights, his face a blur in the darkness. He still hadn't said anything. He leaned closer and brushed her hair back from her face. His fingers traced down the side of her face to gently touch the pulse of her neck. She felt it give a treacherous leap, as he lowered his mouth on hers and kissed her gently. Jenny raised her hand to push him away, but somehow almost of its own volition her hand curled around the back of his neck to pull him closer.

The kiss went on and on. Jenny tried to remember the reason she had been so upset with Wayne that morning, but the warm mouth on hers evaporated her resentment and any memory of anything apart from the completeness of being kissed. She could feel her mouth softening and opening under the insistent demands of that kiss, and the dreamy lassitude spread over her. Wayne was the first to pull away.

'Being nearly burned alive seems to have thawed you out very nicely, Jenny Wren,' he whispered.

'Oh,' she gasped, and cold sanity returned with a rush.

She removed her hand from the back of his neck as if it had been stung. She had actually encouraged him to prolong that kiss. She stared at him through the darkness, aware of the startled thudding of her pulse. The wave of heat rose to burn her cheeks.

'It was a pleasure,' he drawled, as he released her and she made her escape from the car.

A small figure sitting on the verandah rail eyed Jenny with disapproval.

'Where have you been, Jenny? Daddy went out searching for you ages ago. Nobody seems to be going to bed tonight.'

'See you in the morning,' Wayne promised as he drove off.

'Where's he going now?' Merry pouted. 'Why is your face so red?'

'It's past your bedtime,' Jenny said, instinctively putting a hand to her burning face.

It had been a long and exciting day, and too much had happened. She couldn't cope with Merry's questions as well!

CHAPTER 14

There was something different about Taralon, Jenny decided the next morning. She stood on the verandah after breakfast and looked around. The house, stables and outbuildings all looked the same, but there was a difference.

Suddenly she realised what it was. Every single person on the property was smiling. Mrs Harris hummed to herself as she slammed the dishes around the sink. The boys ran off for their school bus without a single bickering dispute. Bill Williams, who came in late from wherever he had been, had a cheerful smile all over his tired unshaven face.

Ben went past leading Pretty Boy, and winked broadly as he saw Jenny. She smiled back. It was so easy to smile this morning.

The suspicion of complicity in the rustling of the stock and the doping of the horse, had been removed.

By now, everyone of the far flung neighbours knew about Jenny's efforts to alert the countryside by starting the grass fire, and the Bickertons' doping of Pretty Boy, and their involvement in the largest cattle stealing combine in the state. Jenny grinned as she thought about the mysterious grapevine of the country district. Even Mrs Harris was full of the details of the Bickertons' brief period of freedom from the overnight country cell, and the passports and airplane tickets found on them.

'I heard they got one of those expensive city barristers to defend them,' she said with a sniff. 'I bet they manage to wriggle out of all the charges lighter than anyone else. Those Bickertons always get things easier than anyone else.'

Taralon settled down again, but Jenny felt curiously unsettled. Bill Williams was brisk and efficient as he took over the running of the property, and gradually the tired haggard look faded from his face. Wayne Paterson hadn't dropped in at all. Mrs Harris mentioned vaguely she had heard he was trying to finish the renovations on the cottage, and she supposed he had a lot to catch up after being away so much.

The weeks slid past and still no one had seen him.

'Breaking up at the end of the week, and no more English lessons,' Allan gloated one night as the two boys and Jenny sat at the kitchen table with their homework.

'You still have to finish this batch,' Jenny ordered. 'Think about verbs as doing words.'

'Doing, done, I hate it!' Allan sighed as he underlined the required words.

Jenny sighed. She definitely was a country person she decided. Her job finished with the school holidays, which was exactly three days away, and she was going to miss this peaceful place and the quiet friendliness of everyone.

She wondered why Wayne hadn't dropped in. For some reason his absence gave her a desolate feeling. Mrs Harris wasn't saying much about him these days, and Jenny got the idea that everyone seemed to be watching her out of the corner of their eyes. She sighed again.

'You want to get yourself to bed early, Jenny Wren,' Mrs Harris ordered. 'You sound tired to me. This heat is a lot to cope with if you're not used to it.'

'I'm thriving on the heat,' Jenny protested.

'Suppose you are looking forward to getting back home,' Mrs Harris probed.

'Yes,' Jenny agreed flatly.

Somehow she couldn't raise any anticipation about her homecoming. Her mother would be pleased to see her, but then her life would settle into a future which suddenly seemed bleak and boring. Jenny sighed again. Perhaps she was tired. She would have an early night.

Once in bed though, the depression settled more heavily. She tossed and turned as she tried to get comfortable. The least Wayne Paterson could have done, she thought crossly, was have the decency to drop in to apologise for his actions.

She punched her pillow into subjection, and wished it was his head. He had taken advantage of her and kissed her when she was still too shaken to fight him off. Except she didn't want to fight him off, the logical unsympathetic corner of her mind pointed out. The slow tears started to trickle down her cheeks. She definitely was very overtired, she told herself and squeezed her eyes shut tightly and concentrated on black poddy calves jumping over ledgers until she fell asleep.

Friday night at dinner she told the assembled Williams family, she would be packed ready to leave in the morning. Bill Williams looked upset, and Merry and the boys set up a horrified clamour.

'Ease up you kids,' their father yelled. 'Jenny Wren will come back and visit when she's got the time.' He looked a question.

'What about after Christmas while the kids are still on holidays?'

'I might have another job straight away,' Jenny said, 'but I will certainly accept the invitation and see you all again some time.'

'Have to get Wayne to come over and drive you back,' Mrs Harris said thoughtfully. She looked at Bill Williams. 'You and the boys had organised to repair and paint the roof this weekend.'

'If someone drops me across at the station, I will get a train down,' Jenny said hastily. She wasn't sure whether she wanted to spend those long hours alone with Wayne on the drive down.

'Rubbish,' her employer declared. 'Wayne brought you up, he can deliver you back. I'll give him a ring later.'

After breakfast, Jenny sat on the front verandah drinking tea with Bill Williams and Mrs Harris. Her hair was pinned up in a neat chignon, and she was wearing her slack suit. Merry clutched her tightly, her face screwed up into a sulky pout.

She was going to miss all of them, Jenny thought to herself as she watched the boys playing cricket in the cleared space below the verandah. She looked down at the sulky Merry, and smoothed a hand over her face, and most of all she was going to miss Merry.

'Here's Uncle Wayne,' Merry said, interrupting Jenny's reverie.

Wayne fought off the boys' welcome as he got out of the car, and tossed the shrieking Merry high in the air. This morning he looked well groomed and assured as he put Merry down, and came up the steps.

'Ready are you Wayne?' Mrs Harris said enigmatically.

'Quite ready,' he said with a grin. He nodded a greeting at Jenny, and picked up her cases. 'The question is whether Jenny Wren is ready?'

'I have been waiting for the past half hour,' Jenny said coolly.

'Come back soon, Jenny Wren,' Bill Williams said. He stood up, shook her hand and kissed her cheek.

'Make that very soon, Jenny,' Mrs Harris smiled as she also kissed her.

'Give us a kiss goodbye,' Jenny coaxed kneeling to Merry.

'Come back straight away,' Merry demanded as she flung her arms around her neck and clung tightly. 'In fact, don't bother to go.'

This raised a laugh from the assembled watchers, and then Jenny was waving goodbye to them all as the grey car drove up the winding track, and out the entrance of Taralon.

'We haven't seen you for a while,' Jenny said, trying to break what seemed to be an awkward silence.

'Just pottering around,' he drawled. 'Did you go back and see just where the entrance into the paddock turned out to be in daylight?'

'By the creek,' Jenny remembered grimly.

'Where it curves around to join the river up from Panniken Bend.'

'Yes,' Jenny said.

At the time of the mysterious attack on her down the river, she had been standing across the river almost opposite to the concealed entrance. Someone must have got very nervous at her standing on the river bank gazing across at the heavy screen of trees opposite.

If it hadn't been for Wayne, the attacker would have succeeded in silencing her, despite the fact she didn't know anything. She gave a nervous giggle. Wayne's brows came down in a black bar, and he reached over to imprison her hand.

'Tony said he didn't intend everything to get so out of hand, but the Combine had them in pretty deep, and they were in real trouble if they didn't play along.'

'Was that his idea of an apology for abduction, imprisonment, and attempted murder?' Jenny snapped.

Wayne's brows flung up into surprised arches, and Jenny noticed that when he smiled he had a dimple in the very centre of his chin. She fixed her eyes on it. It was odd she hadn't noticed it earlier, but maybe he had never smiled so broadly before. She tried to pull her hand away, but he had it securely held. She wondered if he could feel the clamminess of her palm, and the treacherous quickening of her pulse.

'It sounds like quite an adequate apology to me,' he drawled.

'So attempted murder and abduction are the only acceptable reasons for giving an apology around here,' Jenny demanded.

Wayne appeared in a very good mood, but for some reason Jenny was nervous. It occurred to her he hadn't apologised for any of his actions. She sneaked a look at him from under her lashes. Perhaps he didn't consider he had done anything wrong?

'You're a deadly female, Jenny Wren,' Wayne said. He let go her hand and concentrated on his driving.

The car crossed the main highway and turned off it and into a winding dirt track.

'This is not the way home,' Jenny said.

'Just a little detour,' Wayne drawled.

He turned the car into a winding avenue lined with trees, and drove along until they opened out into a protective semi-circle about the house. Jenny's gasp of pleasure was involuntary. The house slept in the sun like a perfect gem. It had been lovingly restored in the colonial period, with sheltering verandahs all around supported by graceful pillars, and edged with iron lace. It had French windows opening off on to the verandahs, and a heavily carved front door surrounded by stained glass, with the motif picked up in the top of all the French windows, and the line of upstairs windows.

'Paterley,' Wayne said. There seemed a hint of awkwardness in his voice. 'It's only a small place.'

'It's beautiful,' Jenny said, realising how inadequate the comment was as she admired it.

She followed him through the front door, and through the echoing empty house. All the boards had been lovingly stripped and glowed almost golden.

'Kitchen and bathrooms are thoroughly modernised,' Wayne explained. 'I don't know how my grandparents coped with all the inconveniences of that era.'

'You were brought up here?' Jenny asked. She paused to look in one of the back bedrooms. It was empty except for an Edwardian rocking horse, shining with new varnish and paintwork. 'No,' Wayne explained. He leaned against the door and studied the rocking horse. 'My father commuted to the farm. My mother was a city lady, so Gwenda and I were brought up in Adelaide.'

There was a silence. Jenny started to feel nervous. Why had he brought her to see the house? Wayne straightened and looked at Jenny. There was a wry smile on his mouth.

'You can stop waiting for an apology, Jenny Wren. I'm not sorry I kissed you. I just got carried away. I was so scared when I realised it was you inside that burning shed.'

'You couldn't have been as scared as I

was,' Jenny shivered.

Wayne chuckled, and pulled her into his arms and tilted her face up. 'Have you ever thought of developing a nice streak of forgiveness?'

'Maybe I would have to if I had too much to do with you,' Jenny admitted. 'What about your friendship with Marise?'

She thought again how secure and natural it felt to be tucked up against him. Almost as if she belonged with him. She tilted her head back willing the feel of his mouth on hers, but he was murmuring an explanation.

'The rustling started six months ago. We thought the animals were just straying, but soon realised they were being stolen, and selectively, by someone who knew which were the most valuable animals. Gwenda suspected our free spending friends were the key to it all. She wanted to discover who their outside connection was. She appointed herself as Marise's constant companion and when she died I took over.' He smoothed Jenny's hair away from her face. 'She wasn't my type anyway.'

'Who is your type?' Jenny asked.

'You're very slow today, Jenny Wren,' he whispered, and lowered his mouth on hers. 'Do I have to put you back into a burning hut before I get any cooperation.'

'Cooperation for what?' Jenny stammered, even as her hands crept around his neck, and she willingly cooperated in that lingering kiss which went on and on.

'Don't give me a hard time, Jenny Wren,' Wayne said wryly, lifting his head at last. 'If you don't agree to marry me, and very smartly, the Taralon mob will have my hide, and what about my reputation? Stop fighting me and leading me on simultaneously, at least until after we're married. You've got me all confused.'

'That will do for starters,' Jenny said in her most docile tone.

The black bar came down over his eyes and his arms tightened painfully. 'Why you...' he began.

Jenny tilted her head back and laughed.

Wayne loosened his painfully tight grip, and gave her a rueful tender smile. The warmth and happiness spread until she felt as if she had champagne bubbling through her veins instead of blood, and her body glowed with the pleasure swirling through. The shadows over Taralon which had blighted her life for so long were now completely gone.

Jenny stood on tiptoe to kiss him again. 'I'm a bit scared of disappointing the Taralon mob too,' she agreed meekly.

This Large Print Book for the partially sighted, who cannot read normal print, is published under the auspices of
THE ULVERSCROFT FOUNDATION

THE ULVERSCROFT FOUNDATION

... we hope that you have enjoyed this Large Print Book. Please think for a moment about those people who have worse eyesight problems than you ... and are unable to even read or enjoy Large Print, without great difficulty.

You can help them by sending a donation, large or small to:

The Ulverscroft Foundation, 1, The Green, Bradgate Road, Anstey, Leicestershire, LE7 7FU, England.
or request a copy of our brochure for more details.

The Foundation will use all your help to assist those people who are handicapped by various sight problems and need special attention.

Thank you very much for your help.